PRA

MW00809663

"Every new da Silva is a dopamine hit. I was excited going in, but this collection really surpassed my excitement. *Infinity Mathing at the Shore and Other Disruptions* is such a carefully constructed mosaic of stories where unique, seemingly individual pieces come together in this emotional amalgam of growth, transformation, and longing, in their loveliest and most terrible definitions. "Grotesque and splendid", the quotes say, and that is precisely what the collection delivers. Satisfying, thrilling, and a read you won't regret."

— ALEX WOODROE, AUTHOR OF
WHISPERWOOD AND EIC OF
TENEBROUS PRESS

"*Infinity Mathing at the Shore & Other Disruptions* is the best kind of collection. It cuts you open, crawls inside your chest, and lives with you long after the book is finished."

— CAITLIN MARCEAU, AWARD-
WINNING AUTHOR OF *THIS IS WHERE
WE TALK THINGS OUT*

Infinity Mathing at the Shore & Other Disruptions

M. Lopes da Silva

CONTENTS

"And yet there was a kind of large splendor about her – absurd though she was, she was splendid at that moment – grotesque and splendid, like some primitive thing conceived in a turbulent age of transition."

— RADCLYFFE HALL, *THE WELL OF LONELINESS*

"While the universe destructs it also constructs. New things emerge out of nothingness. But we can't really determine by cursory observation whether something is in the evolving or devolving mode. If we didn't know differently we might mistake the newborn baby boy – small, wrinkled, bent, a little grotesque looking – for the very old man on the brink of death."

— LEONARD KOREN, *WABI-SABI FOR ARTISTS, DESIGNERS, POETS & PHILOSOPHERS*

IN THE FALL

bully me "boy!" they call me
teeth bare I fight
and love the fighting, red-lipped
bloody boy, nothing else
but a boy, knocking boys down
we fall together
we fell together
we were together   once

INFINITY MATHING AT THE SHORE

THE SURFACE OF THE WATER WAS ALL FRACTALS: symmetries rotated and rotating, pinballing around in the dark. Reed stood at the edge of the pier, his vape exhalations dotted and dashed away by the slow rain. His dark hair curling like a wave. Fredric stood next to him, their hands deep in the pockets of their denim jacket, watching him watching the water.

The pier was empty. The museum shuttered. The diner was missing most of its signage and seats. The arcade had been gutted for its games and prizes decades ago. Reed and Fredric had squeezed through a generous gap in the sagging chain-link fence down by the road, holding back flaps of mesh for each other with rusty chivalry. The old parking lot's asphalt was pierced with weeds, gangly and surprisingly tall like teenagers. Reed and Fredric had woven past them, dots of rain invoking tarry petrichor. Then came the salt, the brine-sick smell of the sea. The startling bulk of rotten wooden timbers in the Pacific tide, groaning and trembling.

Fredric remembered the first time they'd gone to the pier as a kid. The gusts of salty air had thrilled them as they stood by their mother's car and listened to the distant crowds ahead.

They'd loved going to the museum. The neon lights and electric noises of the arcade. The faux 50s décor of the diner.
Running their finger along red vinyl, French fry salt mixing
with strawberry malted in their mouth. But even back then
Fredric had never liked looking very long at the water. There
was too much of it in the sea, doing too much at once. It made
them uneasy.

They'd returned for Reed – of course they had. Fredric
had followed him into abandoned hotels, a couple houses, even
a prison once, always keeping the shot steady and in focus, the
microphone recording at a good level, Reed's face in the frame,
not too much headroom, perfect. Even when they weren't
supposed to be watching him they watched him. Reed's face,
unremarkable except for the fact that it was Reed's face, and
Fredric knew every wrinkle and cis sprouting beard follicle on
it. They should be sick of his face by now, or at least a little
bored of it, but they weren't.

The arcade was just a room with a rat's nest in the corner
now, pinkies squealing in the light of Fredric's phone. The
diner's emptiness was airbrushed with fly shit, rusty chrome
columns offering discomfort where seats had once been
stationed along the counter. Not much there to photograph.
Not even interesting graffiti. A dud of a day so far.

Fredric took the phone out of their pocket and framed the
shot: Reed gazing out at the sea, the clouds big and gray
behind him, his vape the thing most concretely separating him
from Victorian romance.

"Doesn't it frighten you? All that infinity mathing at the
shore," Fredric asked.

The left side of Reed's mouth smiled, a little acknowledge-
ment that meant he knew the camera was back on. "No, I don't
know. I know that you hate it. It definitely makes me feel
small. Insignificant. Maybe it is a little frightening sometimes.
But I like that fear, you know? I like that feeling of being in the

presence of something unknowable, something mysterious and more dangerous than I am."

"You like that feeling? Why?" they asked.

"Isn't that why you come here, too?" he retorted.

"I came here because you invited me," they said.

"Right. But you keep coming back to these kinds of places. It's not like you have to go."

Fredric hears the unspoken thing, too, the thrill hidden by Reed's on camera gravitas: you keep coming back *to me*. And as much as they liked looking at Reed's face they suddenly had to look away, found themself staring at the water. Arcane patterns that only complex equations could decipher carved the brackish murk. Water was self-similar; simply itself in its molecularly smallest and largest forms. Only the names of water changed: drop, ocean. And in its smallest drops, life seethed; radiolarian-rich and fractal.

Fredric was cold, intensely cold all at once. They shivered.

"Just the museum left. You want to warm up?" Reed asked.

Fredric licked the edges of their chapped lips. "Yes," they said.

THE MUSEUM DOORS were already open, the lock rusted away. It was easy enough to sidestep the faded cautionary tape left flapping in the wind, trickier to mind the sudden gaps in pier planking that appeared, warping the museum floor into wild angles, a checkerboard pattern of wood and dark water below. Fredric was careful to capture footage of the ocean busy beneath the floor, its frothy spit regularly shooting up from below to rot the visitor information desk. The museum was a roundhouse, dusty and high-ceilinged. The windows along the walls were tall, shuttered; but the wood on the shutters had relaxed its vigilance enough to allow random lines of light to enter through the fallen slats. It was difficult to capture the beauty of the decrepit space in one shot, but Fredric kept trying.

Reed said something. He frowned at Fredric.

"Sorry, what?" they asked.

"Are you getting this?"

He gestured behind himself. On the landward wall a mural had been painted – a muddled palette of black and blue – mimicking the depths of the sea. Chalky outlines of something Fredric couldn't quite make out were traced over the blue. The mural was bordered by the thick broken glass of a massive aquarium, curving around a stage studded with sculpted rocks and dead barnacles. The water had long been drained from the tank, but a few mucky puddles lingered in the gritty substrate at the bottom.

Fredric aimed their camera lens at the mural, at Reed making his way inside of the broken tank to examine one of the chalky figures on the walls.

"What is it?" Fredric asked.

"It's an anglerfish," Reed said, "Do you know how angler-fish fuck? It's pretty gross. I think you'll like it."

"No. How do they do it?"

Reed's face in close up, the shot so tight around him they could almost touch the frames of his glasses, the smirk of his lips.

"A male anglerfish bites a female, and then he just slowly starts to dissolve into her. Their tissues fuse together. The male's eyes atrophy – his mouth – everything about him changes, becomes purely about physically satisfying her need for sperm as he transforms into, essentially, testicles. And they share one circulatory system – one heart – that female and her one to eight males that she's absorbed."

"You're right. I love it."

HE TOOK the camera from Fredric, but was careful to keep recording. Something for himself, later; Reed liked to collect these moments between them. Souvenirs of Fredric at their most vulnerable, giving the most. Reed said he liked to look at them, and when their arguments went long and nasty and personal he liked to summon the videos up on his phone and remind Fredric of just exactly how much he could destroy.

They craved destruction. That was why they kept coming back. They desperately wanted parts of their own body to atrophy away. How many nights had they longed to wake up the next day with their dick and testicles withered off? Just a few pieces of shed skin lost in the sheets – something to clean out with the next load of laundry. Reed said he understood, but they knew that he didn't. Not really. They wanted him to understand.

They craved rebirth. They wanted to dissolve into him; they have always wanted to dissolve into him. To lose the boundaries of their body inside of Reed. To exist: single-bodied, lone-hearted, twin-brained. Secure locked inside one of the chambers of his heart.

There was a gap in the floor. The ocean wild below. He placed their hands on the twisted metal bar of a safety railing, parted their anatomy, and made them place their faith in iron. Their body swung out over the water as Reed went deeper, harder. Their hands trembled.

The waves of the Pacific Ocean, slick-backed and leaping, were a whale holding all whales in their belly. Alive. Seething, rich and teeming with life. Liquid trembling with nervous systems. Reed's fingers were in their hair, around their throat.

It wasn't enough. Damply they were brought to the ground, to the gritty substrate that crunched beneath them like a rattle. They laughed. They were still giddy with death, with the vision of the water swinging up like vomit. Reed wasn't done – he was lost in himself again – muttering slurs as he dug his thumbs into Fredric's abdomen. Cold sludge was beneath them and they tried to squirm away but Reed pushed them down, back into the old, thick water.

The cold damp iced through Fredric's flesh with every thrust. It twisted through them painfully, set their whole body aching. Every cell in them screamed awake. They stared up at the ceiling of the roundhouse, painted bright blue with sun-puffed clouds, and threads of rain leaked from the simulacra above to break apart on their face. Reed's features were contorted, the gray hairs sporadic on his scalp stark now in the shadows. Fredric frowned; there was something wrong with Reed's face.

They knew every crease, every angle of his features, and his face had changed – was changing – while Fredric kept watching. His musculature and fat were gone, leaving only thin skin stretched across bone, and the bones were rapidly collapsing inward.

"Reed," they said, or tried to say, but his hands closed over their throat again. Too tight: Fredric heard their pulse drumming in their ears like the rain, falling and falling. Reed's fingers dug in, claw-like, and drew blood. Storybook clouds soared overhead.

Fredric ached. Their chest throbbed in time to their pulse. Their legs. Their belly. Their groin. Ice danced in the dark of their nervous system. Fredric's skin swelled with new liquidity, engorging their flesh. Reed was diminishing, his mass receding, his bones compressing, dissolving, becoming anew. His fingers withdrew from their throat because his arms could no longer reach their throat.

Fredric gasped for air and touched the new body that they were becoming: tangibly real. A fact of flesh, full-breasted. They rolled onto their side, attempted to get up, but they were connected to Reed, awkward and ungainly, and fell back down again. The planks of the pier groaned beneath them.

It was all wrong – they had wanted to dissolve into Reed – and yet the fact of his dissolving, his absorption into Fredric's body, didn't it prove a kind of innate feminine quality to their anatomy? Weren't they, too, like the female anglerfish, reducing their lover to his basic physical components of sexual servitude? And wasn't this destruction, this rebirth, something that Fredric had always longed for? The thrill of these thoughts rushed through them, dangerous secrets with all the logic of a dream.

Reed's face was a nubby suggestion of a face, his nose smeared away, his lips a sealed fleshy seam. His eyebrows were gone. But Reed's eyes were still there, two orbs, unblinking, his black pupils ringed by perfect hazel.

Fredric looked away. They kept turning, struggled to get on their hands and knees. Substrate fell from them with a clatter. Moaning, they could sense the perimeter of Reed's body settling into a new, strange shape behind their shoulder blades. Something more portable. Something with two limbs and a tail. They realized that they could feel his body now; his nervous system had intimately entangled with their own and his sensations were theirs. They extended one of Reed's limbs and it unfolded, new bones groaned and unfurled the snapping wing of a manta ray, naked to the rain's chill. A shiver of fear ran through them and Fredric wished that Reed was there to hold them and he did, somehow; they felt the muscular pressure of being held invisibly enfold them. A warmth. A comforting slither of motion pumped inside of them, quick and sure, and another emission of semen dribbled down their legs.

They braced against the glass wall of the aquarium and stood. The pier groaned beneath them. Fredric wept. They felt so beautiful. Life was rich with imperfect blessings.

Fredric took another step, and the floor gave way. They

plummeted, sinking into indigo ink. The water was every-where, tidal, insistent.

They extended their wings. Their long tail thrashed the murk. They could feel all that infinity inside of themself, screaming like an echo.

THE BETTER BOY

As parents, they'd been pushed to the very teeth of their patience before, but on holiday at the cape, with the sand that smelled like iron all around and the languid pressure of sunshine like a thumb on their necks, their anger went sideways into a game.

Harold lifted his lips from his teeth first, beginning it: "Now, the Michael I know, the Better Michael, *he* wouldn't have steered his brand-new, very expensive toy directly into the trees after I specifically told him not to do that."

Diane lifted her cocktail from the wicker table at her elbow, jangling the ice as she sipped. Michael looked at the dirt, his face red with unshakeable heat.

"I didn't mean to, Dad – "

"The Better Michael I know would take responsibility for his actions, and not make excuses." Harold interjected. The insects were sawblade-loud in the sunlight. Michael glanced up at his parents, but their eyes were unreadable shadows behind the violet lenses of their dark glasses.

"I'm sorry," Michael said in a very small voice.

"That's *better*," Diane replied, smiling, and the adults laughed. Michael kicked at a clot of pebbles by his feet, sending a stray one zinging towards the wicker. His parents flinched.

"Hey!" Harold snapped. "What the hell is this? Go to your room right now!"

"I didn't mean to!" Michael wailed. "It just happened!"

Harold stood, grabbing his son's shoulder hard enough to make him wince.

"My son does *not* talk back to me!"

INSIDE THE WHITE shell of the vacation house bedroom, gradually bluing into evening, Harold's words echoed and re-echoed, whispered by the seven-year-old boy who kept spinning the propeller of the model airplane he held rhythmically, mechanically:

"My. Son. Does. NOT! Talk. Back. To. Me!"

If he was not Harold's son, who was he?

This was the thought, sickening, unbidden, and burning behind the boy's eyes in the dark. He suspected that he already knew the answer: the clues had been there, sticky and clinging to his parents' suspicions during the school year. That boy he kissed, Nick; the one he'd been forbidden from ever seeing again. The page with his name on it had been torn out of Michael's composition book, but his name still haunted the pages below. A long hoot of an owl hushed the mourning doves. He could still hear the shore beyond the thicket, and the distant, cartoonish cries of seabirds that made it through the dense branches. Michael preferred the crisp wails of sirens, the clear-cut bursts of car horn rage and street-slung epithets he was used to; nature made him feel unnatural.

MICHAEL WOKE up in the hot darkness, panting. He couldn't seem to steady his breathing for the longest time and panicked, wondering if he was having a heart attack like Grandpa Oak had last year. He remembered Grandpa Oak's hands, with sturdy blue veins beneath the skin like eyeshadow that Michael had seen on the lids of a girl at his school, once – two blue arches above two black circles.

In the casket Grandpa Oak lost his blue veins. Michael had looked at the dead man's hands, right at the places where the veins should be, and his forefinger had darted down to touch before he'd really thought about it. He'd swiped along the ridges, and felt the soft, cold slickness there. Harold had yanked Michael away so quickly from the casket that the boy ended up banging his elbow against it, and giving a short scream.

"I can't believe my son would behave this way!" Harold had seethed. Everyone had been looking, their eyes turning to stare, hungry for anything else but more dreary weeping. Michael's face had gone hot. The eyes made it worse, somehow. Michael's forefinger, the one that had touched Grandpa Oak's hand, went numb. At first Michael worried that he'd touched some kind of numbing poison left behind on Grandpa Oak's skin, but eventually, after sitting in the car a while, the numbness wore off. He'd looked at his fingertip, dirty with the mortician's makeup. Not poison in the end, just paint.

He held his hand over his heart, feeling the awful, twitchy beat of it. He was still alive; not a heart attack after all. He still heard the distant scratch of the shore, now accompanied by the muffled laughter of his parents from somewhere downstairs. There was a skinny yellow rectangle of light beneath his bedroom door. He blinked at it.

Michael realized that he'd missed dinner. The night was star-shot indigo through his windows. His head was heavy and ached in time to his pulse. Michael's stomach gurgled sourly, and he could taste the sudden acid pit the back of his throat.

He stilled his breathing, straining to listen, trying to hear the words he wasn't intended to hear.

"Michael, you're so hilarious!"

The boy froze, the skin on the back of his neck puckering. He couldn't have heard his mom say that – not "Michael" – not his name. Fresh heat flushed him. The cups of his ears prickled as more fragments came through the woodwork:

"The best! – no, I wouldn't think of – you really are the best, darling – that Michael? He's asleep. He's always been a bit – "

Michael squeezed his eyes shut and turned away, cramming his fists against his ears. That helped, but there were still sounds coming through – squawks and groans all bass and throaty treble – and Michael's anger strained at him like the teeth of a stubborn dog, steadily tearing him apart until the scream tumbled out all on its own.

Feet pounded up the stairs. The door was thrown open, the light switch turned on.

"WHAT THE HELL IS GOING ON UP HERE?"

Michael wept. He didn't care that Dad was angry; he was almost glad for the anger, and how it propelled his father towards him. He squinted up through his tears, cringing gratefully as the tirade came. It felt reassuring, almost nostalgic to have his dad by his bed again – Harold's long, monotonous speech was gently reminiscent of a story.

MICHAEL DIDN'T LIKE SITTING in the living room with the broken pieces of the drone placed on the high lip of the mantle; he sensed the presence of the object blazing like a live coal at his back, even with the couch between them. But he still sat on the floor in front of the television set, stubbornly hunched over his cereal as he stared up at cartoons. He was only allowed an hour of cartoons a day, so Michael pored over them with severe intensity.

"It's like you're taking goddamn notes," Diane said. Michael flinched. He hadn't heard her enter the room. He didn't reply to her, because he knew he wasn't expected to say anything.

Harold came in, buttoning up the front of his linen shirt. "He ought to be out running around like a normal child. I know he can run – I've seen it."

Michael tried to focus on what the cartoons were saying. Sometimes it was difficult to tell what was being said if you just stared at the mouths, because the mouths were either too blobby or simply not drawn the way mouths really moved. They never seemed to have enough drawings to go around for things to start making sense.

Harold looked out the window. "Oh! There he goes now! There's the Better Michael!"

Michael swallowed the cold lump of soggy cereal in his throat.

"Stop it!" Diane said, lightly swatting Harold's arm, but she said it in that jokey, insincere way that meant it was still fun.

Michael stared at the mouths. He suddenly felt as if he were miles below his own body, suspended by only the thinnest shreds of his being. He wondered if it were possible to die this way, to suddenly drop dead from falling down inside. Michael tried to imagine his parents at his own funeral – stricken, weeping – but the picture wouldn't come. Diane had only lightly dabbed at the corners of her eyes during Grandpa Oak's funeral. Harold had been angry.

Sweat broke out on Michael's flesh; his parents wouldn't cry at his funeral. They'd be only too happy to give his room to another, better boy.

"Ugh, what is that?"

"Damnit, Michael!"

The cereal kept coming up out of his stomach, and despite his best efforts Michael could not keep it in the bowl like his father told him to.

♂ₓ ℀

"I apologize, Michael. The joke wasn't funny."

Michael didn't know what to say. He didn't think he was allowed to say anything.

"I'm sorry, too," Diane added. "We let it get out of hand. That's not fair to you."

His mouth was papery.

"Well, aren't you going to say anything?" Harold asked.

"Honestly, Michael," Diane muttered, then added, her voice abruptly bright: "What do we say when someone apologizes to you?"

"Thank you for apologizing," Michael answered, the phrase coming to him like a historical date, memorized for an upcoming test.

"That's better," Diane said; only she wasn't joking, probably.

♂ₓ ℀

He was forbidden from running down the tempting stretch of long, golden-green grass that ended up bordering the road to the beach. Lyme disease risk, Harold said, his eyes gone pinkish at the edges. So they walked along the rocky asphalt spit beside the grass, paired off on orders from Diane to "make up and be friends for the rest of this trip". Michael tried to smile as much as possible, to seem eager to be with his father, but it just made his face hurt.

"Do you hear that knocking sound?" Harold asked. They stood within the thicket; the sea roared.

"Yes."

"Do you know what it is?"

"It's a woodpecker," Michael pointed up at the brown mottled bird, tapping on the trunk of the tree just above them.

"That's right," Harold smiled, "it's a woodpecker. But not just any woodpecker, Michael. That's a special one."

Michael swallowed – his throat still raw. "What do you mean?" A brine musk hung in the air, muddled among the scrubby pines.

"That one's knocking on doors, waiting for something to come out."

"Oh." Michael looked away. There was a lingering feeling that he was still far away, and hadn't come back yet. Like he was hollow, lighter than usual.

Harold scowled. "It's a ghost story, kid. You know, oogey-boogey?"

Michael made a sound that was similar enough to a laugh to satisfy his dad. Harold smiled and patted Michael's shoulders. "See? I knew you could take a joke. You've got a sense of humor, after all."

The conversation went on, and Michael did his best to follow it, but even when they reached the beach and the foam went up like fireworks against the rocks he couldn't help but think that he thought he'd seen something darting away, far back into the green and the trees of the thicket.

Michael sat in his room, staring out the window. He'd opened it, even though he usually kept it shut. Having the window open made it easier to hear the knocking of the woodpecker – sometimes near, sometimes far.

The boy twirled the propeller of the model airplane in his hand. It was a Grumman Goblin; he remembered painting it with Harold last summer, in their kitchen. The entire dining room table had been commandeered for the project and covered with newspapers. Diane had made them lemonade, and built a hangar out of a shoebox while they tackled the plane. It had been a very good day – maybe the Best Day.

Michael blinked. He'd seen it again; a figure darting through the trees, just about Michael's size, but too far away to clearly make out. He was absolutely certain that he'd seen it.

He suddenly realized that he couldn't hear the knocking of the woodpecker anymore.

HE STOOD IN THE KITCHEN, staring out the window.

"Hey!"

He flinched, turning to the speaker. "What are you doing in here? Zoning out?" Diane held a fish and a long, thin knife in her hands. As he watched, she delicately began to dismember the animal. Silver scales soon studded the metal sink like jewels.

Time was cut up that way, into pieces. The kitchen—

"THE BETTER BOY NEEDS A BETTER FAMILY!"

Harold and Diane stood, stunned, their expressions long and frozen beneath the electric light of the living room. Then suddenly they were speaking, saying so many words, so loudly and so quickly, he could only stare at their mouths. Even then, it was impossible to get everything right. But no, it wasn't impossible. Nothing was impossible for the Better Boy. He got everything right. Always.

The hand on his shoulder came, firm and unescapable. The Better Boy didn't want to escape. He wanted to get closer. The moment arrived – Harold's arms around him, a joke of a hug, a hilarious turn of events – a kind of game, fun for everyone to play. So he played along, the smile stretching his face so painfully that tears came to his eyes. Everyone was crying, they were laughing so hard. Everyone was crying.

The smell of blood was a lot stronger than he'd realized, as pungent as saltwater. It filled up the sudden empty space.

When it was all over, the boy sat down in front of the television set and turned it to a station with cartoons.

A YOUNG BOY ran barefoot through the long, golden-green grass, a model airplane held aloft by one hand grubby with fresh and scabbing blood. The insects droned and the shore crackled, but not a single woodpecker could be heard.

NIGHT OF THE LIVING GLITTERATI

As THE FREEWAY CUT CLOSE ALONG THE GREEN
Disneyland of Forest Lawn deer stood, chewing their way
through the bouquets on the gravestones, unconcerned with
the vehicles barreling nearby at speeds that could paint their
guts across the asphalt mid-swallow with one elbow jerk.

"Oh, deer!" The comedian said. The actor sitting next to
him blinked in surprise at the suddenness of it all: the
monotony of traffic and trees abruptly replaced with looming
deer, the animals picture book-perfect and bending down to
feast among the dead. The joke. She laughed at the joke Jerry
had made because even though they'd driven past them half a
minute ago the deer were still standing there, in her mind, and
she preferred to laugh at her fears instead of shrieking
them out.

She was just starting out in the Industry and that laugh,
her signature laugh, was her money. She maintained her vocal
chords faithfully with gentle teas, long nights hunched over an
electric facial steamer, performing recommended singing exer-
cises copied from videos online even though she couldn't sing
on key. The singing wasn't the point, the maintenance of the
stretchy threads of flesh within her was.

"They scream, you know."

"What?" the actor asked.

"Deer. They scream. Make all kinds of weird noises," the comedian said.

"That's not very funny."

Jerry laughed. "I'm not on the clock until we get there."

"I guess that's fair. Thanks for driving," she said.

"You're welcome for driving. Hey, who are you now anyway?"

"What do you mean?"

"I mean your name," he clarified.

"We went back and forth with the studio for a while. We eventually decided on 'Marlene'. Just 'Marlene'," she said.

"That's a good one. Classy."

"I like it."

They drove into the sunset, a toothpaste squiggle of gold and burnt orange against the indigo. Then off the freeway, into a four-way intersection and the hills. A digital billboard played a commercial for car insurance: a cartoon car was rear-ended and its cartoon engine burst into two-dimensional flames. The van in front of them jerked to a stop. The comedian had to brake hard. Red light spilled everywhere. At the edges of the redness, shadows moved from left to right. Nothing in the street-lit gloom was distinct.

"What the hell?"

"That's why I asked you to drive," Marlene said. "The streets in this city are a death trap."

A DOE TUGGED on a wreath of chrysanthemums, freeing a blossom. Slowly she chewed the cluster of petals with silver glitter spray-glued to them. This was not the first bouquet she had eaten that day.

Each grain of glitter was a six-sided scalpel, cut to sparkle. Beneath still lakes and ponds the grit of glitter collected into toxic sludge. It remained there, untreated; an unwanted silver lining in the water table. Holographic poison, developing like a negative in the dark. Ready to purge up from the deep with the next stage of the water cycle.

The deer consumed the flowers. Swallowed. Peristalsis pulped petals, and the glitter began its whirling dance within. Esophagus and stomach alike were bleeding, subtly.

This was when the deer would usually start to die. When infection would seize its opportunity. But in the sudden cutting soup of internal hemorrhage – blood and bacteria and polymer blade – a newness occurred. A benison.

Homeostasis.

Not the usual, expected death: not the bleed out. This was an inspiration of biological production, a new solution applied to an old problem. Cells clustered around polymers. Bacterial flocks tended by long viral shepherds feasted on the melee and became part of the newness. The doe staggered among the graves, making a low, guttural sound. The other deer watched her warily, still chewing.

She raised her neck up to the sky, her jaw slack, a long, thin line of saliva sparkling in the last few wisps of the setting sun.

Sparkling too much for saliva.

THEY DROVE past a fancy gate designed to keep Hollywood out of the hills, in stubborn denial of the fact that Hollywood was the hills. A security guard in a blue puffy jacket waved them through.

"Maybe it was somebody with a shopping cart," Jerry said.

"Maybe," the actor said. The comedian had been making

suggestions about what they'd almost hit for the last three and a half miles. Marlene looked out the window, at the multimillion-dollar homes growing dimmer and more suggestively shadowed the further they got away from sea level. Some of the low lighting schemes reminded her of old movies, the black and white ones that they used to print on silver as thin as a postage stamp.

She was still stuck in stucco-land; her paycheck never rescuing her from perpetual rental. There was always a landlord. Always a deadline to make. Always an email to answer and a sketch to write and a video to shoot. Always a plumbing problem and a crack in the foundation and maybe a few roaches, depending on the weather. Something for one of Marlene's girlfriends to complain about, maybe, if she could keep a girlfriend around long enough to listen to her complaints.

"Maybe it was a cockroach. A big one," Marlene said.

Jerry laughed. "And people say I'm the comedian!"

THE PARTY WAS GOING at full speed. A guard at the door crossed their names off of a list on an iPad. The house looked like social media, pretty but so clean that it looked like cruelty, like you could feel the strain of a maid's calves as they teetered to dust the top of the trendy wall décor, their hands splitting to bleed in bleaching agony. The interiors were very pale even at night, beige and bloodless as vampires. Uncultured because no culture was permitted there except whiteness and beigeness. In half a minute Jerry'd left to go talk to some guys he knew from sound design before he had to go outside to work the microphone that they'd set up, and Marlene was left with Lou, a producer from the television show she was currently on who wanted her to meet Elon Musk, an investor. She was already tired.

"Aren't you that billionaire?" Marlene asked, shaking Elon's hand.

He laughed. "The word is out!"

Lou laughed, too. Marlene realized that the billionaire was looking at her expectantly. Like he wanted something. She could read it in the twitch of his eyebrows, the slight widening of his eyes into a prompt.

She took a deep breath, and unleashed her signature laugh. People clustered in nearby conversational groups hushed a little, to listen to her laugh and smile fondly at the sound. Elon smiled, too. Marlene felt ill, but she kept laughing.

That was when the screams from outside started up.

Marlene's laugh left her. Phones were fished out of pockets and purses and poised to film the unknown source of the chaos, aimed roughly at the dark beyond the stylishly tall glass walls. Silhouettes of palm trees and hedges were recorded. Muffled shrieking. Then a shape, angular and amorphous, spidered out of the dark towards them. It connected with the thick glass. A heavy crash harmonized with a fae tinkle of breaking glass, and the screams from the outside were suddenly dragged indoors.

A stag was standing in the hallway, breathing heavily.

Injured partygoers, lines of blood redrawing their designer drip, stared at the creature in awe. The animal loomed above them, shards of glass shedding from his fur as he walked. The deer had no eyes. Instead, the stag's eye sockets roiled with holographic glitter that wept into his fur like disco tears. Everyone watched the animal, rapt.

The stag raised his long, majestic neck up, exposing teeth that sparkled like a thousand red carpet gowns, and then began to vomit glitter upon the assembled glitterati below.

The toxic plastic sludge sprayed the wealthy guests, who

screamed at its burning touch. Marlene watched as Elon's head disappeared underneath a wash of polymer vomit, particolored and pretty-pretty, his shrieks of pain garbling into gurgles and then nothingness.

She laughed.

Again and again and again. The stag vomited and thrashed, mingling with the panicked partygoers. The animal kicked an infamous director in the chest and spewed holographic puke on his face. An actor renowned for his rigorous exercise routines and tough guy roles rammed into the deer's side and tried to wrestle it to the ground, but as his arms grappled with the stag's mass the animal turned and took a rainbow-toothed bite out of his neck. Blood arced gracefully from the gap. A guard took out a handgun and shot at the stag. Glitter exploded from the wounds like blood squibs for a robot on a kid's show. The stag kept going. And now there was a doe.

"A female deer," Marlene sang to herself, so far off key she would never be able to get back on it again.

WHEN THE DEER came down from the hills they entered directly into the city's streets, paved and bustling, and the traffic that pushed through the arteries of asphalt coagulated around this fresh chaos. Cars and people collected around them, stopped their cars and took out their phones and hoped to capture something that might change their lives.

Deer vomiting glitter, that was something to see, maybe; then later, maybe something for the authorities to deal with. But badges weren't glitter-proof. Cops littered the pavement like craft projects. Animal control's tranquilizer ampules were ineffectual. Bullets like blowing kisses.

Like the mountain lions, like the coyotes that snatched

neighborhood dogs and cats away in their jaws at night, in time the deer were accommodated for. Normalized. Another local joke: gotta love those fucking glitterati! They're crawling out of the woods now.

A new homeostasis in Los Angeles had been created.

BODY OF THE SPOREBEARER

"Do you want to do mushrooms together?" they ask me, and I want to admonish them for spending the money on our pleasure, but I think this could be a trans masc thing, puerile associations between mushrooms and phalluses already sprouting in my neural nets, so I nod like a good young man and dilate the sphincter of my gullet obediently to ingest. They delight over the new opening of my orifice; a bird spying the grub of my tongue. They kiss me, slipping particulate between my lips. The musty, wooden leather of a mushroom restrains my palate. I kiss them while we wait for impact. For the shuddering apart of everything that I suspect will come. But time shaves off in small curls that I trace along their neck, modest and steady. I spiral with them, slowly. I descend, and, in the act of falling, begin to ascend.

I notice the growth along my legs first – pale pins plucking free from flesh – each new sprout a solemn ecstasy. Tiny fruiting bodies bearing tiny fruits. The bloom encroaches on my forearms and the scraggly dark triangle beneath my chin. Soon I am full-throated, bearded, spongy and spore-dust powdered. My chest and belly tingle with fresh growth. I twist and crane my neck to see it better. They keep kissing me, and I worry about spreading infection to them, but they are fearless and suck the tips of my new strands clean. I become erect, my T dick responding to the sounds of their meticulous attention. My Skene's gland, swollen, spurts swiftly to soil us. We sit in that moment, stunned, merely breathing. Waiting for our lungs to let us speak again. They run their fingers lightly over my moisture and fresh pins erupt at their contact. They aren't finished with me yet. I am ready for whatever happens next. I am here.

I AM RECEIVING NEW MESSAGES. Tiny thoughts, joyful and bright, speckle my anxious inner drone. Yes, I am terrified of dying, but what if I am not alone? What if I never have to be alone ever again? They hold my face with hands larger than my own. Wiser than my own. Their wisdom is a gentle warmth, softly seeking me. Eager but undemanding. Our eyes, upon meeting, become Our eyes: I see what they see, and likewise. Invisible golden flesh wires us together tenderly. Our vision, thus united, is reluctant to break apart. Any subtle fracture of our eyeline would be an injury, immediately felt. We both know this because the message has been clearly delivered. There is no static on the line, only pure tones. A smooth umami clings to our palates. Dirt forms in the small, secret bowls beneath our tongues. It spills out from the sides of our mouths when I smile.

IN THIS LIMINAL space there is no distinction between us. There is no fixed conscription of roles such as "teacher" and "student"; we teach each other. We learn from each other. To claim ascendency would be a strange fascism in this languid idyll. Neither of us are willing to do it. We will remain equal in our undoing. Both of us kings or none of us kings; either way will do. We will decay together, serenely. Violently. Tearing the rebar and each other apart.

THEY SMILE and push me down. The carpet beneath me becomes me. Concrete crumbles and bends. The Earth unfolds. I hold them close when the world gives way. We are subsumed, sheets of dirt pulled over us, disoriented but not dead. Grit presses against us, every grain potent, empowering. I am quite happy to be in their arms, in the dark, our teeth bones grubs that gently tug at my new growths. They're feeding now, but they'll save some of the mushrooms that they harvest to sell online tomorrow. There's still bills to pay, this is no utopia; but I'm delighted to know that I am nourishing them inside and out, that my body will keep us fed and housed. That my presence will sustain us both for a bit longer, just a little bit longer while my fruiting bodies try to tear this system apart. I'm confident that all we need is some more time and we'll make it.

NEON

Bright blue claws sank into the dinosaur's neck, which immediately began to ice over: the first step in Icepick's classic decapitation combo. I held my breath in anticipation, waiting.

My brother's thumbs rolled across the yellow buttons – up-down-right-right-left – and the dinosaur thrust a stick of live dynamite into Icepick's ribcage. I started breathing as she screamed. Lines of hot pink pixel blood splashed across the screen. "YOU WIN...THIS TIME" popped up in tall white letters over the pink. A kid I didn't know well from my brother's class clapped a couple times. Two other kids hooted at my brother to quit while he was ahead. The crowd around the Neon cabinet was always thick.

"Let me have a turn!" I shouted, fighting the bass-heavy rumble of the game as it growled next to me, so close there was a tremble in my ribs. "You said I could and Mom's almost back. Let's do two player mode."

My brother grimaced, his braces flashing metal. When he spoke, he leaned into his disdain so hard that I could feel his words bend beneath the sudden weight. "I'm in *tournament mode* and I'm almost at *ghost level*. Wait it out, dweeb."

I frowned, twisting on the dirty toe of my high top. "This always happens," I said, but this time my brother just listened to the game.

"Select a player," came from the speaker. His thumbs moved. A square box traveled over a dense grid of different names and faces: a fox-headed character with a sunset reflected in its shades called Foxfire; a flaming skull attached to the body of a heavyset wrestler called Pyro; a metal-studded cyborg with the head of a T. rex called Dinomight.

"Dinomight sucks!" Someone heckled, and somebody else giggled, but my brother clicked once, twice, and Dinomight was confirmed. Again.

He never picked my favorite, but then, nobody did. That was why I had to play her. It was important.

But now Dinomight was on the screen, facing off against Foxfire on the top of a building. Behind the characters, the skyline of a city glowed, thick with flying cars that looked like the edges of axes as they cut by. When the soundtrack kicked in my excitement grew, even though I wasn't the one playing the game. The synthesizer had a weird organic sound to it, like a dampness clinging to the notes that always creeped me out a little. Everyone went quiet; nobody had gotten to the ghost level on Neon at our arcade yet. A red "5" appeared on the screen. The countdown matched the rhythm of my pulse.

"Where's Lexy?"

"I dunno. I haven't seen her for a couple days."

"That's weird. I thought I'd find her here."

"Yeah, me too. It's funny because Neon finally came out."

"Yeah! That's why I thought she'd be here. She couldn't stop talking about it."

"I haven't seen Eric, either."

"He was pretty excited about Neon, too, wasn't he?"

"Yeah, he likes fighters. And this one has a lot of hype."

"Maybe he just went back to live with his stepmother again."

"Could be."

I turned to see who had spoken, but I couldn't tell. The kids were all staring at my brother's back and the screen beyond, their faces switching in blank unison from red to purple to gold. I frowned.

"Explosive! Explosive! Time to blow up!" Dinomight's attacks, like all of the Neon fighters', came with terrible catch phrases.

It was funny that it had been almost a full week since Neon arrived at the arcade, and nobody had gotten to ghost level in tournament mode yet. Not funny like a joke, but funny like the joke was on you. The arcade was always packed after school, and on weekends it was so busy that our parents never let us go. Theoretically, somebody in the Saturday crowd should have topped the tournament board already.

It was possible, though unlikely, that everybody had been scared off of it. Neon was a violent game, one that we had been specifically told not to go near after the local news ran a story about it. But the game also had a reputation for being tough to play – a game for true fans of the arcade world – which is why my brother was obsessed with beating it. His initials were all over the screens at Funtimez, and the untouched tournament board on Neon's screen was just the sort of challenge my brother loved.

And what was that empty space to me? A dream I wasn't allowed to have.

I looked at the fluorescent yellow face of my cheap digital watch: 3:46 PM. Mom had wanted us waiting outside the arcade by four.

"YOU WIN...THIS TIME," the cabinet growled.

"Dale, let me take a turn," I said.

"Grow fungus!" My brother said, which was something he knew grossed me out.

I kicked the side of the game, hard.

43

"NEON IS WATCHING YOU," came from the speakers.

"What was that?" I asked, suddenly nervous. We hadn't heard that one before.

"Look," Dale said, pointing at the screen. It had gone black, with the four words "NEON IS WATCHING YOU" glowing in pink. Suddenly, the words began to lose pixels, dissolving, becoming something else, until two pink digital eyes formed.

Some of the kids whistled, others clapped.

"GHOST LEVEL!" boomed from the speakers. Kids cheered. Ten conversations started at once.

"The game is supposed to study your play style the whole time, so the ghost level is like your ghost – a copy of you," I heard a girl explain to her friend.

"DINOMIGHT SUCKS!" yelled the heckler, quick to double down.

"Eat shit, Carter!" my brother shouted back. Apparently, he knew the heckler. Dale confirmed the selection of Dinomight, and the screen went dark.

And then our mother showed up.

It was chaos. Kids laughing as Mom's hand clamped down on my brother's shoulder to spin him around and the lecture began. Dale's angry gestures getting bigger and bigger until he ended up mashing the button panel by accident and the screen froze into a looping twitch of abstract digital snow. Us getting escorted out, politely but firmly, by a manager in a sweat-spotted dress shirt as the 'out of order' sign was taped to the Neon cabinet by a teenaged employee.

"Wow, Dale. Just, wow. The language, and the game I specifically told you not to play – and right in front of your sister!"

"Okay, so ground me," said my brother. "I'm already dead."

"Oh, you're not dead yet, mister, but you are definitely

grounded. Two weeks! And nobody allowed over at the house."

Mom hadn't been paying attention – it had been months since Dale had invited anyone over. He didn't say anything, though. I stared at him. There was something different about him. He looked out the window, his face slack as if the anger had completely left him already. I couldn't tell what he was thinking at all.

I squinted. The edges of Dale were a little fuzzy, some-how. It felt like I had a floater in my eye, and I blinked a few times. Dale turned, scowling at me.

"What are you looking at?"

The lights reflected on the curves of his eyes were perfect squares. I grew cold.

"Nothing," I said.

HE WAS LOSING RESOLUTION.

The edges of him were jagged, forming steps instead of curves. But when I tugged on Mom's sleeve and asked her if she thought he looked any different she stared at him for a long time, then said: "He's growing up so fast he's going to need new jeans before the back to school sales hit. Maybe we can go to the Bargain Bin next weekend."

Nobody else noticed.

I WATCHED Dale stand in the yard.

I was supposed to get him – to have him come in and get ready for dinner and help set the table – but he was standing in a far corner, his back to me. In the deep yellow-red of the sunset, I saw what he'd really become.

Twitching, there and erratically not-there, the shadow of a cyborg T. rex superimposed over my brother's body. Pink ropes of electricity crackled soundlessly across the impossible pixels.

He turned to look back at me. His neon eyes met mine.

"Dinner!" I blurted, looking away as I slammed the back door.

THE FIRST KID confirmed dead was somebody I didn't know – a sixth grader from the middle school Dale went to. Our parents tried to keep the gory details away from us, but we found them out eventually: the police weren't willing to call it a murder because it looked like the attack of a wild animal. Warnings were announced on the school PA systems, telling us to avoid wooded areas and travel in groups.

Those warnings didn't help Carter. They found his body in the woods. But they couldn't call his death an animal attack like the first one because of all the burn marks they found.

I tried to talk to Dale about it, but he wouldn't respond. He just grinned a little and when he did all I noticed was how *long* his teeth were; how jagged.

NOBODY ELSE BELIEVED ME.

Dale was a pain, but he was my brother, and I had to do something. This had to stop.

I showed up at the arcade with all the quarters I could find in the house jingling in my pockets.

"Hey, aren't you supposed to be in school?" Said the bored teenager poking through a horror comic book at the register.

"I'm home schooled," I lied with a confidence I did not feel. But even though a cold sweat clung to my scalp, when I looked back, the teenager had returned to her comic book. I was a little disappointed in her complete lack of interest; I had the tiniest of crushes on her.

The arcade was quiet. It was just me and the employee at the register. The Neon cabinet still had a handwritten "Out of Order" sign taped to it. I pulled the sign off of the screen. The machine was on, noisily flipping through its demo of fatalities.

I pulled out a quarter and selected "1 Player", then "Tournament Mode". The character selection screen came up. I stared at the grid of glittering choices, shining like a wriggling treasure horde. I pushed buttons, moving the golden selection box across the animated faces. Click-click-click – I stopped when the square wreathed Icepick.

Icepick was everything: everything I loved, and everything I wanted to become. I wanted to look like her. To quip like her. To worship her. To fight like her. To kiss her. To marry her.

I broke out in a sudden sweat that I scrubbed my palms free of along my jeans. Taking a deep, shaky breath, I selected her.

"*Nice pick*," she said, her pixel mouth twisting wryly at me. She was in on the joke. I loved that.

"Thanks," I whispered.

The screen dissolved into the starting scene for the first fight: an ambiguous purple-bricked alley covered with posters for fake bands and musicians (David Wowie, Uh-Uh, and Truck Halen were the ones I could read the best). A sparsely-animated crowd watched from the shadows as Icepick faced off against the first challenger, Toughpuff, a humanoid cloud with inflatable muscles wearing a bright orange pair of shorts.

The countdown started, and my guts grew cold. I thought about my brother, and his uncomfortably long teeth. I stared at the screen. Icepick was so wonderful, and I didn't want to disappoint her.

"...one! Fight!" The cabinet commanded. I pressed the buttons.

I lost in under a minute.

I looked at the carpet, mad at myself. Of course I'd lost; I rarely got a chance at the controls. It made sense that my coordination was off. But still.

I put another quarter in the machine.

And lost again.

I kept going. This time, I got to the second level. I tried to remember all the combinations I'd seen Icepick perform when my brother played against her. I still couldn't figure out her decapitation finishing move. I should have spent my allowance on the fighting game magazine I'd seen at the drugstore last week promising insider tips. I hadn't had enough time to memorize it all in the checkout line.

I lost again. Back to the alley.

The first hour sped by quickly. By the end of it, I was getting smoother with her. Almost in sync. I didn't have to consciously think about the buttons anymore, at least. But it still wasn't good enough. I lost again, my heart breaking as I heard Icepick's death wail. I stuck my hand in my pocket and wiggled my fingers: my quarter horde had been whittled down to two, and I wasn't even close to reaching ghost level yet.

I closed my eyes.

Ghost level was hard because the game watched your moves and learned from them. Like how I'd watched my brother play for all these years, as he hogged one video game controller after another. Observation was powerful.

I opened my eyes: I *knew* all the moves already. Winning was about predicting your opponent's decisions, and then outmaneuvering them. It was a guessing game, played at the speed of a button-click. An endless roshambo.

Easy.

I opened my eyes, steadying the shake in my hand, and put one of the remaining two quarters in the Neon slot. I selected Icepick. As the numbers began to count down against the purple bricks, I felt oddly relaxed yet hyper-aware at the same time.

"...one! Fight!"

I cleaned up Toughpuff quickly, finishing with an uppercut spike of ice that impaled the cloud-humanoid through the chest, leaving a still-beating heart quivering on the frozen tip. Icepick's hair flicked in a silver arc over one shoulder.

"Cold-hearted," Icepick said with a wink and a victory pose.

The screen went black.

"NEON IS WATCHING YOU," growled from the speakers, the words appearing on the screen in electric blue letters. The words remained on the screen for a long moment before becoming two solid blue eyes, glaring at me.

"*Icy* you, too," I grinned back. That wasn't even one of Icepick's lines.

The rest of the levels flew by.

"GHOST LEVEL!" thundered from the speakers.

"Hey, what's that kid doing on the Neon machine? That's out of order!" I heard distantly. I hunched over the cabinet a little, fresh sweat forming on my upper lip.

"Get that kid offa there!"

I remembered my brother, flailing against the cabinet, and raised my hand up.

"Hey! What the heck is she doing?"

I smashed the buttons, hard. The screen froze. Icepick looped and twitched with digital distortion, mid-kick. Once. Twice.

I blinked. My eyelids glowed with inverted pixels. My right hand spasmed with sudden motion. I heard a curse and quickly-approaching footsteps. I ran. My high tops pounded across the spaceship-patterned carpet, onto the gray tiles of the shopping mall. My muscles burned and flickered with a weird rhythm – almost painful, then not-painful, then numb, then an ache of the numbness wearing away – repeating over and over again under everything became a burning blur. I looked down at my hands and my fingernails had become thick, clear and faceted.

I couldn't stop smiling.

$$\mathcal{P}_{\times} \, {}^{\circ}\!/\!{}_{\circ}$$

My brother stood in the living room, completely obscured by the towering digital form of the cyborg dinosaur. I knew he was in there somewhere, though, the same way that I now stood inside of Icepick's seven-foot frame.

I flicked Icepick's long silver tresses from our shoulder as blue light sparked and writhed around us. It felt wonderful. Dinomight laughed, exposing his long, jagged teeth.

"Icepick sucks!" he said.

"Cold reception," I said, and hurled a bolt of ice and raw power at him. He dodged, rolling aside from the attack, and it hit the wall instead, freezing a framed photo of me from kindergarten.

"Mom isn't going to like that," he said.

"Who cares?" I shouted, my voice united with the deeper, melodious tones of Icepick's. "You killed those kids! You need to leave my brother alone, right now!"

Dinomight grinned. "Time to BLOW UP!"

I threw up an ice shield, narrowly blocking the sudden shards of our spontaneously combusting television set and coffee table. Mom wasn't going to like any of this. I had to finish him quickly.

I threw back my right hand, feigning the uppercut

required for a Cold-hearted finish. Dinomight blocked it: just as I'd anticipated.

I reached for Dinomight's throat with my left hand, high above my brother's five feet, and sank Icepick's frozen claws into the cyborg's flesh. Ice instantly collared the digital neck with a crackle. I grinned.

"Brain freeze," I said. Dinomight's head frosted over. With a twitch of my fingers, the cyborg dinosaur's head snapped off, spraying gore-slick ice shards as it bounced on the ground. Cerise blood pumped from the headless neck in square-edged gouts.

The digital silhouette flickered away with a snarl of hot pink static. Then it was just my brother standing there, swaying on his feet as he slumped forward.

I caught him before he hit the ground, holding him in Icepick's long, muscular arms.

My heart trembled. I smiled, and Icepick's blue lips curved along with mine. I didn't even care about what Mom might say anymore. The sun was setting. I felt the night collecting in the sky over the distant city like a mist, heavy and cold. It prickled on my new skin. I couldn't wait to get out there and play.

COAGULATIO

It's a joke when she grabs my breasts from behind – just a joke! – and she's telling me how much I lack compared to her abundance and when my eyes meet hers in the mirror and my heat starts burning her fingertips she squeezes and says:

"You're just a baby."

And she lets me go. And I am in graduate school but I can't think of what to say to prove her wrong. My age is not the obvious qualifier that I thought it was. I ask for my bra back. I need to get dressed. We have class together in half an hour. Her apartment is so far away from the campus that her boyfriend will have to drive us if we want to make it in time.

I put my sandals on, the ones she constantly teases me about wearing, and start to walk to class. She yells at me about it. Gets the boyfriend to drive his banged-up sedan alongside the curb while she shouts at me to get in for half a block. I ignore her. I remember last night even if the beer wore off her edges again. How I'd been the lightweight as usual, and she'd rolled me into her bed and arms so neatly I was asleep within minutes. But I also remember him lurching in later, booze-thick and wanting to crawl into bed with us and his intentions, and how her arms had caged me then and she'd shouted him back to his bottles. I'd leaned into her torso, the base of my neck nuzzling the growl from her chest, and known a perfect thing. I'd felt it, purring and warm and ready to tear a human apart for my sake. It was in her pulse, in the slightly sticky sweetness of her skin. And I'd wanted more but all I'd been able to do was keep snuggling against the heat of her until unconsciousness took me under again.

The baby. The lightweight. She's the one who always invites me over after class and starts pouring them into me as if that were the only way to get me into her bed. I keep ignoring her. The boyfriend drives away after a while.

I'm going to be late for class today. Maybe too late for the one after that, too. And the headache from my hangover is starting to hit me like I took its money. I need water and painkillers. Probably food. I only have five bucks on my ATM card and three singles in my wallet. If I touch the card, there will be fees. I'm in that gutter of time where I usually stay home and eat ramen as much as possible; I don't get paid until next week.

THAT's when I see them.

In between two buildings, back where a small parking lot abuts a dirt slope, they kneel over a wide-eyed white woman lurching away from them, her designer denim blotching into a puddle. Tears are in her eyes, sliding down her face. I want to help her. I look around but nobody else is on the sidewalk. The storefronts are still caged up. There's only me.

I step forward, thinking I'm going to scare them somehow. Make a lot of noise. I take a deep breath, and that's when I really look at them.

They're wearing a long black coat that is covered with silvery things that I think are sequins at first, but they're not. They're actually mirrors, each edge easily sharp enough to draw blood. I try to study them clearly, but the only thing I can see are the mirrors and my own reflection made myriad.

"Do you see me?" they ask.

And I look at their face but can only make out the silhouette of their hair, kept shorter than I cut my own. Everything else is piercing light and reflections. Myself multiplied. A dazzle I cannot see beyond.

"No," I say.

"Unfortunate. Are you afraid?" they ask.

Despite the woman trembling on the ground beneath them, despite my inability to perceive their face, in this moment I am not afraid at all. I am filled with a sense of inner elevation. Recognition even, poignant and golden in the gut. I am lit with wonder.

But there is also the woman, weeping at their feet. She doesn't get up and run away even though she could. She just stays there on the ground, shaking. Yes, I am afraid.

"I wasn't afraid, but now I am," I say.

"Interesting," they say. And I can sense them looking at me even though I can't see their eyes.

But then they return to the woman, bend low over her, their face only inches above her weeping. I want to stop them but I'm too afraid, too fascinated to intervene. Some sick part in me wants to see what happens next.

Their features are unclear but their mouth is open, their teeth sharp and abundant. Sharper and more abundant than the teeth typically found inside of a human mouth. They position these teeth above the open mouth of the terrified woman and begin to make chewing motions.

There's cracking, fleshy tearing and the woman writhing below them, but I see no injuries. No wounds. No blood. They growl as they feed, gently. They keep chewing above her, and she cries and screams and wriggles so violently on the concrete that her expensive haircut becomes a suggestion. I keep thinking that the screams are going to bring somebody. One of the houses behind the dirt hill is going to have a resident that will make a call. But nobody comes to their windows; nobody is being a hero behind the skincare clinic and used game store today.

They keep chewing and chewing, and the woman keeps screaming and suffering, and I just watch, nausea and a thrill surging through me until suddenly it all stops.

They swallow their last swallow, rub their knuckles across their closed mouth, and the woman sits up, blinking slowly. She gets to her feet. Stares off into the distance.

She is smiling faintly.

And they are suddenly standing next to me, their teeth so close to my neck I feel the warm pulse of their breath against my skin.

"I like you," they say.

I run.

As fast as I can, my sandals doing better on the concrete than I would've anticipated, I run. Even though they aren't following me into the busy main street, I keep running. Even when I get back to my apartment my heart is still running down the sidewalk, my legs are still running, and they won't stop feeling the miles moving below them even after I turn off all the lights and make myself lie down in bed. Even when I shut my eyes, I'm running. I can't stop running. I can't stop.

I CAN'T SLEEP.

My thoughts are tangled with them. Before I know it I'm touching myself.

I want to sleep in their naked arms, finally free of mirrors and reflections. I want to feel their nose and teeth press against the nape of my neck, the sides of my face. I want to growl when they do, for their rage to reverberate in my ribcage. I want to nestle and lick until our growls become purrs and other, more arcane sounds pretty and primeval and cheap. I let my orgasm pull me to sleep, gently.

They are waiting for me.

In my dream they wear the coat of tiny mirrors, but this time when I look at them, I don't see my reflection broken up into pieces, there is only my face, uncomfortably large and grimacing back at me.

"I want to see your face, not mine. Will you take off the coat?" I ask them.

They laugh. "I can't take it off. Only you can."

I frown. "That doesn't make any sense."

They smile at me now. "I'm not even wearing a coat," they say. Their sharp teeth are the only things I can clearly perceive in the brilliant static of their face. But I can also see the coat. That, and my own face frowning back at me along the surface of it. The face that I usually avoid looking at in the mirror. The face that doesn't look like me.

"Do you love yourself?" they ask.

"What?"

"Well, do you?"

"Sometimes," I say.

"Only sometimes? What a pity," they say.

"I'm trying," I say.

"Trying to do what?"

"Love myself," I say, feeling increasingly silly the longer I speak. "It's just not working."

"Why not?"

I shrug. "It's hard to love yourself. It's easier to love someone else."

Dream-quick they are close to me, sharp teeth poised delicately by my ear. "Is that so?"

I tremble, wanting them. "Yes."

They withdraw. "Then why don't you try loving yourself the way you want to love me?"

I'm lightheaded. The edges of the dream room are starting to move around. "What?" I ask.

But I'm awake. Alone in my bed, but there's a warmth in the empty space beside me on the queen-sized mattress that I have no explanation for. I let my hand rest in the hollow there.

I'm a little lighter. As if a piece of me has been surgically removed in the night. But there aren't any scars or incisions. I'm just...not as anxious as I usually am. It's pleasant.

I ignore the messages on my phone left from Andrew at work. I go through all of the clothing that I own and throw out everything I wore when I was trying to "act like a woman", whatever that was supposed to mean. I want to get my hair cut shorter. I am tempted to pick up a pair of scissors and try to give myself a haircut, but I have heard too many horror stories. I schedule an appointment at the barber shop on campus. I come out as non-binary online, and shut off my phone when the messages start to be a little too much.

I go to class and ignore her. It's easier to ignore her today. I puzzle over their words from my dream as if they were the key to my thesis paper. I don't really hear my art history professor's explanation for the still life that's going to be on the mid-term. The fly-kissed fruit projected on the screen at the front of the classroom looks delicious; I want to devour it directly from the raw canvas. Tear the wet oils free with my teeth. I am so hungry.

There's a needle of pain in my mouth, and I instantly taste blood; my mouth is full of it. I've cut my lower lip on one of my canine teeth. I try to just swallow the blood, but after the third swallow I start to get nauseous. Lighter than flesh should be. Unusually porous. I'm sweating too much. I accidentally catch her gaze and she rolls her eyes at me. My face gets hot and I want to cry but I won't in front of her. I won't be the baby.

I try to swallow the blood in my mouth but it won't go down this time, and when I cough it ends up spraying all over the notes and backs of the students sitting in front of me. One student screams, which starts another student screaming, and soon I am scrambling to collect my stuff and not slip on all the blood that I keep choking out onto the floor. I'm apologizing but nobody's listening. I manage to get my stuff and leave.

I GO BACK to that place behind the skincare clinic and used game store, but they aren't there. It wasn't a great idea, anyway. They had no reason to go back there. I decide to walk around for a while and see if I can spot them again. I'm not going back to the campus today.

I make my way through Los Angeles on foot. The going is slow. The clouds are low and gray and a sharp wind picks up. I start shivering. The next time I pass a thrift store I duck in and buy myself a coat, officially ending my ATM card. There will be fees. But right now I'm a little warmer, and the coat does something for me; I look more like myself. Just slightly, but for now that's enough. Black has always looked good on me.

I keep walking. I keep looking for them. Every shriek of sound grabs my attention, but these are inevitably brakes squeaking, an espresso steamer, screams of delight. It's never them. I walk until everything in my body hurts.

I'm hungry. I spend my last three bucks on a street taco. It's amazing, nourishing and perfect, but I am still hungry afterwards. I'm hungry but my hunger is distinct; I don't want food. I don't want sex. This is new: I want to feed on somebody's fear.

Once I know what I want I'm terrified of myself all over again. It feels like my heart is trying to tear out of my shirt. Even though my legs are burning, shaking, I run. My face is hot. Sweat and tears leak out and they might as well; there's only strangers around to see how much of a baby I'm being right now. Strangers that I want to watch writhing beneath me in fear.

THEY'RE WAITING for me at home. I startle at their silhouette standing in my studio apartment. Then I tremble – not tiny quivers but broad, rubbery shakes. My raw, overworked body gives up on my ability to make decisions and I sink to the carpet, slow, then half-falling there.

They approach me in seconds that pass like minutes. Each tiny mirror winks in and out of the light, teasing a broken piece of me, concealing a piece of them from me.

"Please," I beg them. "I don't want to hurt people."

"You don't want to hurt him?"

I know who they're talking about. "It's not right." I say.

"He would've hurt you."

I look at the carpet. "I don't know. You don't know that for sure."

They place a hand on the top of my head, a hand that burns with static as it makes contact with my scalp. I feel that lightness return, and I'm not afraid to talk about her boyfriend anymore.

"I want him to be afraid of me," I say.

"What else?"

"I'm hungry."

"For what?"

"You," I say. I look up at them, and in that moment, for an instant, there is no coat. There are no mirrors. There is a face, a little like mine, but different –

Then the static rushes back in, the mirrors. The coat. I blink, but I am starting to forget the face that I saw. I panic, a fresh swelling of fear in me, but their hand teases my hair and I am needle-prickling then lit from within again, tranquil and still. Hungry.

"One day you will ask me to eat your fear," they say. "Every last bite. And I will."

New fear quickens my heart, my breath. "Does it hurt?"

"Oh, yes. It is easily the worst pain you will ever feel in your entire life."

"I hate pain," I say, "I'm a baby about it."

They squat beside me, their brilliant prism-skewed face grinning sharp teeth at my own. "Then grow up, baby."

I kiss them and they kiss me back, all sharp teeth cutting my bottom lip and static flaying my flesh to unseen cinders. I offer them my tongue to prick. They oblige and I am swallowing blood again, heady and elevated, sucking on sharp teeth just to hear them groan with lust. I growl at the taste of my own blood and the sound coming from them now is perfect and holy and mine alone. Everything hurts, but I am still afraid; they leave my deepest fears untouched. They will wait until I am ready for them.

They like me, and they're like me.

I SEE her at the Halloween party, by the beer coolers on the back porch. She's a harlequin and he's a clown. Her boyfriend's hand is around her neck again – just a joke! – and he's saying what a pain in the neck she is and there are a couple guys laughing but then they're gone and it's just me as his audience. The party's going on real loud inside the house.

"What are you supposed to be, a disco ball?" he says.

"What are you talking about?" I say.

"Your coat," she says. "it's covered with sequins. Kinda retro!"

"I'm not wearing a coat," I say. I left it at home. I wasn't feeling cold at all.

"Whatever," he says. He won't meet my eyes. She won't, either. She keeps squinting at me. I keep thinking that I have never seen her scream before.

"Keri wants to talk to you," I tell her. "Something about the mid-term."

"Oh yeah?" she says, turns to him. "Babe, I'll be right back." Pecks him on the cheek.

As soon as she's gone my teeth are out. So sharp! So long! So suddenly close to his own! And he is wide-eyed and trembling, his heart rate a tremor as I run my hand across his chest and up to lock around his throat.

Shuddering, I dig in. I eat. And eat. And eat until his bladder voids and his tears come and he is left numb and placid, glass-eyed, a perfect newborn happy for the pap of a beer I crack open and hand him. He spills it everywhere. Suckles the foam noisily from the metal lip. I leave before she gets back.

I DROP OUT OF COLLEGE. Stop answering my phone. Start paying my rent with money from people who have forgotten how to fear poverty. Every night, I look for them. I want them. I want them to see just how much I've grown. How much I've eaten. I want them to eat every last scrap of fear I have left in me while I scream and suffer for them alone. And then, when they have pushed my body beyond its oblivion, when I have given them all of my most intimate pain and I am no longer afraid to tell them I love myself, I want to pull them to me and make them groan as I eat their deepest fears.

THE ONE WHO WHISPERS 'HOLD ME CLOSER'

In thickets dense with wood and lush green they woke, heart quickening with chlorophyll, and the boy's body stirred, budding anew. They were holding the bones of a human, intimately threaded through the skeleton like muscles, and separating from the corpse was slow, melancholy work. It was painful to disentangle. They ached with every effort. The body remembered why they were holding the bones, but the boy in the body was new. He hadn't lived long enough to remember anything. His heart was quick with chlorophyll and love. Spring was coming. He smelled it: a thin musk, livid and green.

Finally they were free of the corpse. Vine-sinewed, wood-muscled, the ancient body craved light so the boy stretched it out lazily, limbs spilling up and over everywhere, extremities curling into leaves so thick and pink they were petals. They were flesh. And the petals of flesh ascended to the sunlight, the corpse abandoned and pulped to powder below, and the ancient yellow human skull that had been a part of their body for centuries now was presented to the sun. Who the skull had first belonged to was forgotten; even the body did not know. The nameless sockets caught the golden glow of the sunlight in their twin cups and kept burning with it, an ancient torch reignited by Imbolc's fire. It was February first.

The boy in the body didn't know anything about calendars or clocks, or why his body had a womb. But he knew the time, and that he was not the first seed to bloom here. His torso was thickly ringed with so many broken hearts, if he cut himself he could count them all. They were dead lines forming his grain. The boy shuddered and the body shook in sympathy. He would not make that cut. Instinctively he knew what love was, and that he craved its touch. He would go and find love for himself.

THE YOUNG ARCHITECT walked along the hiking trail, drawing a house like a tree in his mind, with solar panel leaves and brachial ventilation systems and sewers that rooted responsibly into the earth. An adobe, no, a living kitchen, complete with herb garden and a mushroom shelf. A composting basement. He kept rearranging the living space, never satisfied with his bathrooms. The trickiest thing was to remember the light – an invisible sun in an unlived place – and how to best hold it in a room. Light kept the space alive.

A flicker of gold among the shadows caught his eye. He hesitated. The gold was dappled with pink and green, and the wooden brambles nearby were tangled so beautifully, so intricately, he found himself searching for his phone in his pocket as he left the trail. He regretted not bringing his sketchbook along.

He didn't notice the dirty fragment of tibia that he stepped on along the way.

THE SUN LOVED HIM FIRST: lavishly, wonderfully. The sun spoiled his son on earth. His celestial warmth filled the boy's ancient body with new life. Fresh vines itched and unfurled. Everything was perfect because the boy felt perfectly loved. Only, that wasn't quite true, because there was a small part of the boy, some portion inside of him that could not be reached by the sunlight's love no matter how the body twisted and contorted to catch the light. He didn't yet realize that fragment of himself wanted love that the sun could not provide – a vitamin the UV spectrum did not deliver. He was too young to know.

It was that small part, that tiny inner shadow, that made the boy turn away from the sun and face the forest floor where the architect stood looking up at them.

The young architect was the most beautiful being the boy had ever seen. Even the sunshine was not as sweet as the wonder that lived in the center of his eyes. The curiosity that burned there was brighter than fire; somehow brighter than the glow captured in the sockets of the boy's skull. Flustered, sap spurted afresh. Buds itched out of the boy's body, pinking his green. The architect opened his mouth as if to speak.

Then came the crashing of the young architect's fiancée among the leaves, her voice calling out his name: "Brandon? Brandon?"

"I'm here," the architect said.

The architect looked back but the boy was already gone.

The architect's arm was looped through the elbow of a young woman with dark, serious eyes. She listened to him as he gestured at the trees.

"I know I had my phone out, it's silly that I didn't take the picture but I don't know, you weren't there. The thing was, I don't even know how to describe it. There was the skull and the, I guess, you see those vines there? A lot of those, and thorns, but, structured somehow into a torso with these scribbles of – you know it was like a sculpture. Like a sculpture that could move."

"Like an animatronic?"

"No, not at all. The movement – goddamnit I should've hit record – "

Hidden far back in a bracken, the boy in the body watched the woman guide the young man back to the path. The skull's jaw canted open slightly with need. Growth was necessary. The body sprouted new air sacs, cornsilk vocal chords, a fleshy palate and thick tongue to slide along the skull's teeth.

"Bran...don..." they said.

BRANDON, too distracted for the soporific release that sex would bring, spent the night awake as Celine slept next to him. He kept fidgeting with the illustrations in his sketchbook – relentless repetitions of vines and skulls – none of them could capture what he'd felt. The lines were too dry, technical when they should be expressive. And the light – there was something about the light that he couldn't quite convey on paper.

Brandon scribbled over the current batch of doodles that he'd made, turned a page, and began again. He drew the wild tangle. The skull that had stared at him with such intensity he'd thought, for a minute –

He wished that he could write poetry, because Brandon wanted to repeat words that felt like a spell, that summoned that moment back to him. That moment when he believed again that the universe was wild and beautiful and loved him as much as he loved it.

Red-faced, he reached for himself beneath the sheets, staring at the marks on the pages he'd made. The image tilted with the rhythm of his need.

IN THE MOONLIGHT the body was stiff and slow and the boy was left with only his hope for company. Still, he hoped. He dreamed, and his dreams were indigo blueprints, and the home he built was the architect's body.

BRANDON CAME BACK. He'd told Celine that he wanted to hike the trail alone, and even though she'd teased him about wanting to spend more time apart from her, she hadn't really objected. The front of the trail was busy this time. Brandon kept passing hikers clutching water bottles, their wrists uniformly adorned with smart watches.

When he got to the bend where he'd seen them, he stopped and waited for a while until the trail was clear. Until the quiet crept back, and the lizards and mice started rustling the weeds. Then he slipped away, angling towards the place where he remembered seeing the gold.

OVER THE PAST WEEK, the boy in the body had grown into a man. He was older now, his need for love more urgent, and more sharply defined. He would not last forever, he knew; he would not know a winter. The green skin of his vines had coarsened, darkened, and his buds were in bloom. He thought often of the architect; he had seen many people travel along the trail by now, but none of them had been him.

So it was like dreaming, like a continuation of the man in

the body's dream, when the architect returned to him. The architect was tired, the edges of his eyes pink with rough sleep.

"You're real," the architect said softly. "I wasn't sure, but you really are."

"Brandon," the man in the body said, his voice like the groan of wind through oak branches.

Brandon stared at him, at the miracle in front of him that somehow knew his name.

The man in the body tilted his torso up so that Brandon could see the fresh petals growing there, dewy and dense around the leaking gash in their chest.

"Are you hurt?" Brandon asked, extending a hand hesitantly.

"Brandon," the man in the body said. He knew no other words.

The architect approached the living bramble, staring at the yellow skull that peered down at him. He looked more closely at the suppurating slash in the wood; it didn't look like an injury after all. The petals grew naturally from the edges of the thin slit. When he touched one of them, the body moaned, a living harmonium.

The man in the body brought his skull close, closer to face Brandon. When the jaw parted, revealing their fresh-grown tongue, the architect found himself opening his own mouth to receive it.

THERE WERE thorns and cries of pleasure embittered with prickles as the man in the body loved the architect. There were new parts to grow – fresh stamens to spend on his lover – but after the holding and being held, the man in the body always let Brandon go. And Brandon would go, his steps light on the trail, a little drunk with love.

If Celine noticed, she didn't say anything, so Brandon didn't say anything. He thought about him. About their body like a stained-glass ceiling above him, breaking the light into ten thousand beautiful pieces. He'd forgotten to take a picture with his phone again, but this time he didn't care.

The spring was full of their trysts. The only thing they wanted was to be together, flesh tied taut to vine, lost in the miracle of finding each other.

Celine started to notice. Not just Brandon's absence, but the results of his absences. The hours he needed on his own stretched into afternoons. Evenings. Camping trips. There were the bruises. Scratches and scrapes that kept getting bigger and healing slowly. When her accusations came Brandon did nothing to deny them. It was easier to be accused of infidelity than loving a miracle.

Besides, he had the man in the body to return to. Brandon was trying to teach him to speak English. He wanted him to choose a name for himself.

Brandon's work for the architectural firm kept getting sent back with enough notes to fill a novella. His designs were labeled "impractical", "uncomfortable", and "inhuman", but Brandon knew that they were examples of the best work he'd ever made. He was drawing houses for gods. For miracles. When the company fired Brandon, it hardly bothered him. They were throwing away real talent.

He chose the name "Christopher", after one of the main characters from the A.A. Milne books that Brandon taught from. Other words, soft and supple, came soon after. Summer's apple trees thickened with fruit and the new seed in Christopher's chest grew heavy. Their trysts became frenzied with a new, strange urgency; Christopher was restless. Something was coming. Things would change. They were running out of time.

At night, the body remembered what was to come, and shared their wisdom with Christopher in a dream.

Autumn's chill would be felt first; their sap would move slower, or become pure shards of ice if a frost hit early, slashing through the body's capillaries from the inside out. On one of these very cold days, when the seed in Christopher's chest was very warm and heavy, Brandon would come to them, and Christopher would want only to hold him very close, very tightly, but this would be the last holding, because once Brandon was tightly secured in their arms the body would sleep the same sleep that it had slept for thousands of years, and Christopher would die.

And Brandon, trapped beneath Christopher's body, would die, too. A long, slow death. The body remembered: ten thousand or more people had been held by the bramble body and their yellow skull during the harvest, and none had gone to them willingly.

Centuries of humans spurning their touch.

Before that, a long, long time ago, there had been other bodies like the man's, and those bodies had mutually entangled with love and desire. The memory of their passing was the most bittersweet of all. It mortified Christopher, those ghosts of antediluvian lovers, their touches the faintest shadows falling across time to cool his spring-quick sap.

He couldn't keep anything from Brandon: as best he could, in the words he knew, Christopher told him everything.

THE ARCHITECT WALKED BACK down the trailhead, trying to remember where he parked. The hikers gave him funny looks and steered wide paths around him. His car had been towed away weeks ago. He'd forgotten that he'd only been wearing the forest floor for over a month now. Brandon fished his phone out of his pants and turned it on. His cell phone still had a charge. A slim red line of battery beneath a broken screen.

He called a ride home.

AUTUMN CAME and Christopher knew that it was time. He hadn't seen Brandon since he'd left in the summer. He didn't know exactly how long it had been, but he could feel the absence like an ache. Like he'd been hollowed out inside and there was nothing left but dying to do.

Christopher was dying. He was stretched thin, about to become another ring in the grain, and maybe this time, without a human's corpse to nourish them during the winter, the body would die, too. Maybe this was the end of all of them. An end to the endless winters and springs. An end to all this yearning.

That was when Christopher heard him.

"Brandon," the man in the body said.

"Christopher," the architect said. Brandon removed his clothing. He approached them but the brambles flinched.

"Don't..." the man in the body said, "I want to hold you."

Brandon reached out and caressed the yellow swoop of zygomatic bone tenderly. "And I want you to hold me closer."

THORNS LIKE NEEDLES sewed them together on the forest floor. The wind stirred the branches above. The sky was such a bright blue. As he slowly died Brandon thought how wonderful it was that sometimes miracles needed to be loved, too.

SATURATED

our grand temples were all cheesecake factories
our priests influencers   our heroes mickey mice
+ you were there   with ketchup stigmata   mustard
halo
mouth open
to bless or curse me i forget

A COCKROACH IN THE BRAIN

Jake Spring "the Earworm King" needed another hit, and he needed it bad. Everything was past due. In the red and bleeding out. The residual checks were down to their scummiest residue; the kind of grease that wasn't even thick enough to hide Lincoln's tomb on a penny, and Jake barely had anything to show for it. The new apartment he'd moved into after the divorce was still empty, just full of Jake and his unpacked boxes. A futon couch. A big flat television set mounted on a wall. A kitchen full of empties and pizza boxes. A grown kid that wouldn't answer his fucking phone calls, no matter how much money Jake funneled to that ungrateful shit's bank account. An ex leaving texts that were goddamn novellas. Jake slugged down another shot of cheap bourbon from a plastic drive thru cup that had never made it to the garbage and ended up becoming a permanent roommate. The paint was so scuffed away it was impossible to tell which drive thru the cup had originally come from. It was Jake's favorite. His chalice.

"Ingratitude is the attitude," Jake said aloud, trying it out. It felt right, the slogan sang; how ungrateful Sandra had been for all of the hours he'd invested in his career, and all of the money that he'd made for them. How, in the act of utmost ingratitude, she'd effortlessly passed that ungrateful gene onto their own child. Left him a legacy of it.

He frowned into his cup. The brat that Jake Spring had spent years loving and raising as his daughter, his precious Daddy's girl, all that was being thrown away now by an adult stranger who wanted Jake to call it "Robert" and "son", and for Jake to "understand" and foot the bill for a pricey surgery? Ingratitude, clearly. A fundamental misunderstanding of what Jake Spring had wanted to foster and leave behind in the world. He had to be clear about these things.

Clarity was the order of the day: the client had given Jake Spring a very firm deadline, and he was already far behind it. The client was furious. Jake had until the end of the night to find his muse or she'd be dragged in and forced to witness his execution, or something like that. Jake laughed aloud at his own bullshit. Nobody else did anymore.

It was five o' clock. He moved the three music files he'd been tweaking for the past six hours into a digital trash can and was rewarded with the sound of digital paper crumpling up in his headphones. The songs had all been stilted, forgettable – DOA. Not the kind of thing a human synapse would summon up while a person was distracted. Not good enough. Not earworms. Nothing now.

Earworms were only partially understood by science, the bulk of their mystery hidden by the coy meat of human brains. Auditory cortexes in divine waltzes with memory. Upbeat melodies, simple to catch onto, interrupted by something unexpected. Words that wormed in. The melodies felt infinite, unending, and human brains, in love with patterns, kept trying to guess what should go next, kept solving the puzzle nobody posed them, one note after another after another leaping onward.

He could steal. He'd done it before: taken a popular melody and ripped the guitar and vocals out of it, rearranged a couple percussion moments and soon it was as good as new, and difficult to legally sniff out the original cadaver. A lot of poppy rhythms were pretty similar, after all, and Jake was a clever butcher.

Jake finished what remained in the bottom of his plastic chalice and reached for his phone. He checked his email again and found something new nestled among the all-caps callouts from his client – a message with a subject line that he hadn't expected.

Fealty for the Earworm King

The nickname was something that he'd given himself years ago, part of the press release packet for a popular dog food company. He'd earned it, too; one catchy jingle of his after another netting millions of dollars in sales. Clients had come running, once, begging for Jake's musical insight. His infectious touch.

The sender was some nothing spambot of an address, a string of numbers typed after the word "muse". There was an attachment, too – all the standard sorts of warning bells and whistles.

Jake opened it. There wasn't anything inside of the message, just the attachment. It was a .wav file titled "whatyouvebeenlookingfor". He scanned it for viruses – nothing. Jake Spring smiled at the screen, invincible with bourbon, and downloaded the file. It immediately opened up on an audio player and started playing.

The melody started off subtle, fascinating, tickling the very exterior of Jake Spring's ear canal, and he understood that this was subaural, recorded the same way that ASMR was commonly recorded, and that the tickling was not unpleasant, and forming a peppy beat.

Jake had just reached for the volume to turn it up when the sound level in the file increased as well, and Jake winced and realized to his horror and fascination what he was listening to: it was the recording of a cockroach trapped inside of a human's left ear, edited into a melody.

The bug flailed, its phantom legs scraping Jake's eardrum into raw bloody holes, and he screamed and tried to stop the playback but the microphone was panning from left to right, in such a steady and deliberate way that the cockroach rhythmically scraped and twitched its way directly through his brain, only to pause just long enough in the right ear canal for another hideous eardrumming.

And it was all catchy. Catchy as hell. A real earworm, and Jake Spring knew earworms.

Jake tried to disconnect his expensive wireless headset but he panicked, he stood and his arms yanked through the air at nothing, slapping his cup away and banging directly into a nearly empty bookshelf. Framed photographs of his family rained down on him, sending Jake to the floor.

The back of his head hit the carpeted concrete of his office floor, but his headphones kept playing the melody into his dwindling consciousness.

Jake Spring's mind memorized, mesmerized; anticipating each note of the insect's journey. It crawled through him, an unknown pop sensation that made him want to claw everything inside of his skull out with his fingernails. The music incubated him; it infested him.

He wasn't supposed to feel this, he was supposed to be booze-numb, untouched; not stuck with this terrible cockroach skittering back and forth inside of his brain. And yet, wasn't this what he was always looking for? Wasn't this a hit, an honest-to-god earworm, and wasn't this the sort of connection that he'd always wanted with the son he didn't want? A part of him hoped that Robert had sent the file, because the bubblegum tremor of the roach's legs promised the Earworm King a kind of forever; a puzzle for his brain to keep solving with dreadful certainty leaping onward and onward.

KNOCKABOUT

Baynor feinted, ducked in close, then aimed a lucky jab that put Kaminski back on the mat. The crowd outside the cage shrieked in giddy delight.

Moreira hit the spacebar on his laptop, pausing the video.

"You see that? Right there? He knocked his Knockabout loose," Moreira said.

Olivier stared at the retired fighter and the video he pointed at, then shook his head and scrubbed the stubble of his mohawk's fade with his knuckles. It was late. If they went much longer they'd mess up Olivier's sleep schedule again. The gym office wore a murky cologne of sweat, urinal cakes, old leather, and cold coffee.

"You mean Baynor hit him hard enough to get an advantage?" Olivier asked.

"No – that's obvious – why would I point that out? I said what I meant: Baynor knocked his Knockabout loose," Moreira said.

"Okay, what the hell's a Knockabout?"

"It's the thing that lives up here, in the birdcage," Moreira tapped the right temple of his own head. "We all got one."

"First time I'm hearing about them," Olivier said.

"Here, watch it again. This time, just look at Kaminski's eyes."

Olivier let his legs bounce in place as Moreira hunted for the point to start playback.

"Here," the retired fighter said.

The action was all the same: the feint, the duck in, the jab, but this time Olivier studied Kaminski's eyes the entire time. Olivier expected the eyeroll, the sudden blanks of white sclera, but he didn't expect the abrupt wiggle, the odd momentary flash of something red that looked suspiciously like a second iris struggling for control of Kaminski's left eye.

"What the fuck?"

"So you see it now," Moreira said. The shot cut away to another angle and Moreira paused the video again.

"I don't know what I saw. Kaminski's eye looked fucked up – was that a blood clot or something?"

"That's his Knockabout coming out," Moreira said.

"Moreira, you can't be filling me with bullshit, man," Olivier said.

"It's not bullshit, it's something to watch out for. Your insurance is absolute crap, and if you get hurt bad, not even winning is going to cover your bills. I'm looking out for you."

Olivier stood up. "Look, it's getting late. You can tell me how shitty my insurance is tomorrow, okay?" He picked up his gym duffel.

Moreira leaned back in his chair, massaging the thick lump of bone in his nose, a souvenir from a break that had earned Moreira a heavyweight title once: his "lucky break". That's what Moreira called it in the story he'd told Olivier time and again in the gym.

"You don't believe me," Moreira said.

"Does that even matter? I'm paying you to believe in me," Olivier said, and walked out of the office.

"I JUST DIDN'T EXPECT this kind of crap from Moreira at this point," Dallas Olivier said. "He's supposed to encourage me, not try to tell me fucking fairy tales."

Dallas's boyfriend laughed, and because his arms were wrapped tight around him Dallas could feel every squeeze of his laughter as it came out.

"What are you laughing at?" Dallas asked.

"I just can't imagine Moreira having the patience to tell a fairy tale to anybody – not even a group of kids," Aaron said.

"That's what you think. He talks about his 'lucky break' all day long. His broken nose and his title. 'Sometimes you have to sacrifice something to get in a winning hit' is basically his catchphrase. He's got the patience of a tortoise."

Aaron shrugged, and Dallas felt that, too. "I dunno. When I've met him I've gotten the impression that he likes and respects you a lot. He talks about you like you're his son when you're not in the room."

"Now you're just trying to make me feel guilty. Too late."

"I take zero responsibility for your guilt."

Dallas leaned back a little more into his boyfriend's embrace. "Therapy has made you far too powerful."

"Yup. And it's given me the wisdom and grace to add that if he's telling you something, it's probably important to him," Aaron said.

Dallas sighed, making Aaron's arms sigh around him.

"So you're saying that even if I don't get it, just listen to him for now?"

"Mmhmm."

"Fine. Now will you shoot me up with drugs?"

"If by 'drugs' you mean your T, then yeah, fine. Go get it. But I'm going to tell your opponent that you're terrified of needles," Aaron said.

"Hey, Halifax can't bring a needle into the cage – I think I'll be okay," Dallas said.

Dallas sat upright to go get his testosterone, but before he could break free Aaron's arms closed in for another hug.

"Yes! Defeated by a hug hold," Aaron said, and laughed when Dallas pushed away in mock offense.

THE WEIGH-INS WERE MESSY. The crowds were loud, and thick with transphobes. Security kept most of them corralled, but somebody in the back threw a beer can. The can was so loaded with beer that it ended up going low and hitting a guard in the face. Beer misted down. Olivier paused, grinned, and held out his hands theatrically, then shrugged. When he got to the stage, he grabbed the microphone from the announcer and said: "Weird weather we're having on Dallas tonight."

A lot of people in the crowd laughed. The announcer attempted to grab his microphone back, but Dallas Olivier kept it just out of reach. A heckler said something else, and Olivier grinned.

"I'm being paid to talk shit tonight, but you're doing it for free, buddy. Looks like I'm coming out ahead of the deal. Enjoy a beautiful view of the parking lot. Yeah, brought to you by those security guards right there," Olivier said.

Olivier handed the microphone back to the announcer, who looked a bit put out. Olivier smiled at him.

The weigh-in itself was a blur of posturing. The owner of the organization showed up and made a little speech about how much he cared about all of his fighters, even the new ones. He was giving himself a lot of points for recruiting "the first trans man to fight in an official MMA organization". Olivier stretched. Olivier's opponent threw a lot of punches at the air and bounced on his heels, going real showy about his cardio training. Ray "Hailing" Halifax had a heavy brown beard that wreathed his scowl, and thick eyebrows above two scornful blue eyes. His eyes were the things that Olivier would have to watch more closely than Halifax's joints or his footwork; the eyes knew the plan first. The body knew it right afterwards.

Meeting Halifax's eyes, Olivier went truly calm. The encounter with the heckler had sparked through his limbs with wiry anxiety, but seeing the man that he was about to fight summoned a different emotion; a primal anticipation of picking him apart in the cage. Of definitively proving his fighting mettle on television. Earning his place in the ranks. He floated in the feeling and stood on the scales, a little dizzy from sweating out three pounds into a garbage bag suit that morning. Olivier just barely made the cutoff, but he made it just the same.

Backstage in the locker room Olivier blew up.

"Why the fuck are they selling those bigots beer at the weigh-ins?"

Moreira shrugged. "You know the owner of this shitshow would sell lighter fluid to an arsonist, why are you asking me?"

Moreira removed the last piece of tape from Olivier's hands. Olivier rubbed his palms together and popped a couple shots at the air.

"Why did you mention that Knockabout crap last night?" Olivier asked.

"I told you why," Moreira said.

"Bullshit," Olivier said.

"I think you should wait for a better opportunity," Moreira said.

"This is the biggest org in the MMA world, and they invited me, an unknown, to fight in their bantamweight division – what kind of 'better opportunity' could I possibly get?"

"One where they give you time to train and study your

opponent, not a month. This is too quick, Olivier. It's a spectacle, not a real match-up."

Olivier held his hands out. "It's always going to be a spectacle until more trans men fight in MMA."

Moreira frowned. "Maybe so, but why go out on their terms? Why not wait until they're hungry for you?"

"I dunno, they seem pretty hungry to me. Why not give them a taste?"

"Because what do we know about Halifax? He's 2-0 and finished in the first minute of the first round with a KO in both. His camp is somewhere in California, but nobody we know trains there. Nobody in Las Vegas has ever heard of him. He pushes buttons and sends guys to sleep on the mat, but acts like he could last in the cage for hours without breaking a sweat. The guys in the booth claim he's studied BJJ, Muay Thai, and wrestling – the standard holy trinity. What does that give you to work with? How do you strategize for 'look out for his fists and maybe don't go to the ground with him'?"

"At least 'look out for his fists and maybe don't go to the ground with him' is something I can work with," Olivier said. "Are you going to give me anything else I can actually use or should I just head home now?"

Moreira regarded Olivier sadly. Rubbed the bony ridge of his nose. "Listen. That time when I fought Alda for the heavyweight championship, I know I've told you about that. And yeah, sometimes you have to sacrifice something to get in a winning hit like I did, but then again, maybe that's just an excuse I'm making because I couldn't figure out a way to beat him without busting my nose open. The only thing I really know is this: sometimes you don't have to give anything up at all. You can figure out another way to win, Olivier. A better way."

Olivier laughed. "When you figure out how to do that, man, be sure to tell me," he said.

OLIVIER STEPPED into a smear of light and sound. He couldn't even hear the song he'd picked for his walk out over the volume of the crowd. He stayed light on his feet, keeping his heartrate up even though he was pretty sure his anxiety could take care of that without any help from him. Everyone was in place. Halifax was out there already, roaming the cage like a restless animal. Aaron was at home watching Olivier on television while working a remote customer service shift. And Moreira was at Olivier's side, guiding him gently towards the cage and the tiger in its middle.

Everything went so quickly. Halifax oozed the same intensity he'd had at the weigh-in. Sometimes it was hard to see his eyes in the glare of the arena lights. Olivier hadn't thought about how harsh the lights would be. How much the light would bounce off of the white, logo-tattooed mat. Olivier frowned. There was a lot of blood on the mat, and their match was one of the preliminaries. He wondered who'd bled out. If he knew the guy. Then Olivier had to touch gloves with Halifax and he swore around his mouthguard at himself for getting distracted by a little blood and glare as the bell called the round's start.

It was the first round of three if he could stay in it. There was the blue of Halifax's eyes – two points of anger hunting for weakness. He was going to throw a right jab; Olivier avoided it. Kept his fists up. It was tempting to drop them and try for something big. To turn Halifax's MO against him, maybe, or attempt a takedown – Olivier ignored the temptation. Kept moving. There was no guarantee that Halifax would drop if Olivier found his button – some people didn't. Halifax threw another punch that Olivier defended. Olivier responded to it with a leg kick aimed at Halifax's right shin. The kick hit with a clean, meaty slap.

Olivier worked the leg, Halifax threw jabs and the occasional uppercut. A couple of Halifax's hits landed, one starting a plum over Olivier's right eye.

Halifax aimed a left jab at the plum. Olivier dodged it and tried for another leg kick. The kick landed, but Halifax grabbed Olivier's leg. Olivier twisted away before Halifax could get a firm hold. Halifax turned his attempted hold into a takedown attempt, his shoulder abruptly shoved into Olivier's gut and forcing him backwards and down to the mat.

Olivier let Halifax's momentum take them down, but slid back to brace himself against the cage. Halifax was on top, but struggling, unable to secure a dominant position. Elbows and wrists rubbed elbows and wrists. Halifax's sweat burned Olivier's eyes as it rained down on him. Halifax jerked an elbow free and slashed open the plum. Blood smeared Olivier's vision and Halifax's arms. Olivier bucked his hips up and threw Halifax free like a bronco. Blood went everywhere. The crowd screamed. The bell rang.

Olivier felt the cutman working over his face as Moreira tried to get his attention – it was difficult for Olivier to focus. Everything in his body was screaming; everything outside of his body was screaming. Moreira looked upset. Olivier tried to smile reassuringly but his mouthguard was in the way.

"Defend yourself – don't worry about being aggressive. I don't like how much he wants to take you to the ground," Moreira said.

The cage doctor aimed a penlight at Olivier's right eye. Olivier winced at its brightness. His vision was better now that the blood had been wicked away, but the eye itself somehow felt raw and overcooked at the same time.

The second round was exactly the same amount of time as the first round had been, but now every minute crawled. Olivier tried to keep the strike exchange roughly even while defending, defending, defending. The freshly-drained hematoma above his eye refilled itself slowly. Olivier waited for Halifax to try for another shoot down to the mat, but his blue eyes were hidden in the glare of the lights overhead and no shoot came. Their footwork was fast, a back and forth sending Halifax and Olivier into wary oblong paths. Apropos of nothing, the plummy hematoma sprang a leak. A blood-and-sweat slurry started to trickle down into Olivier's right eye. It was still okay until it wasn't, and Olivier realized that he'd lost sight of Halifax's left fist which was suddenly making contact with Olivier's right temple.

The bell rang before Olivier fell back against the cage. There was a brief moment of bloodthirsty exaltation from Halifax's fans, but Olivier kept his footing and their cheers turned to boos. Olivier flipped them off and staggered back to his corner and cutman, half-falling onto the stool placed there.

Moreira was talking but Olivier couldn't focus on the words. His vision was being examined by the doctor again. As the penlight flared into his iris Olivier winced. His right eye ached, and for the briefest fraction of time, Olivier's vision doubled over itself, confusingly, like two transparencies placed atop each other just a millimeter out of position. Olivier shook his head and his vision clarified.

"Be careful out there," Moreira said. "protect yourself."

But Olivier knew that he had to make a killing. It was his last chance. Halifax was leading just because he'd cut the plum and one of the judges was always sweet on cutters. Olivier would have to take a risk.

The bell rang and Olivier was in the action, circling, aiming strikes that Halifax easily avoided. The crowd responded to this change in strategy with a surge of low, throaty brays: this was the kind of reckless aggression that they liked to see.

Olivier saw an opportunity for a takedown and took it before he could think about it. Halifax wasn't expecting the move – he was off his feet in seconds – but on the way to the ground he brought his right elbow down on the back of Olivier's head.

Halifax's universally org-banned move came down not just once, but twice, a third time before the ref noticed that Olivier was out and limp in the hold. The cameras got tightly framed, gratuitous coverage of the elbow's descent and the repeated contact it made with Olivier's skull, but no camera was aimed to catch Olivier's right eye jiggling in his socket, twisting round and round until a bright red iris blinked in the place where his brown one had been.

The ref hadn't quite made the call to end the fight yet when Olivier's body stiffened to alertness. His right arm curled back, then aimed a tight, powerful punch directly into Halifax's side.

Halifax's elbow lost its power and glanced sideways off the back of Olivier's head. Olivier threw another punch into Halifax's side, then another. Another. Halifax winced, his torso twitching with each throw as he tried to scoot away, but Olivier hugged close to him, flurrying his fist at the man's gut. The flesh there reddened, then purpled before the roaring crowd's bloodthirsty scrutiny. Halifax struggled to break free but his motions were panicked – keys for no locks. He was trapped.

Olivier sat upright and punched Halifax in the face in one smooth motion. Before anyone could clearly tell if Halifax was conscious or not Olivier gave him some more punches. Then some more. Halifax's mouthguard had fallen out of his mouth, the ref was pulling Olivier away before he popped more teeth out of the unconscious man's mouth, but Olivier was grinning as a mullet of blood streamed from his scalp to his shoulders.

Olivier had won. The ref said he had won, and held Olivier's wrist up in the air, but for some reason Moreira looked as sad as if Olivier had lost the fight and the world was double exposed with something Olivier couldn't quite make out.

Olivier held his head in his shaking, rust-knuckled hands. Moreira's office wore the same stuffy cologne, the odor now spiked with a fresh cup of bad coffee.

"I can't make it stop, Moreira, it's always there. Is this what happened to you?"

"No, kid. I didn't have to make that kind of sacrifice. I've known guys who had, though," the retired fighter said.

"What's going to happen to me? I can't stop wanting to hit. To fucking murder. I can't. It's never been like this before," Olivier said. "I'm scared. Scared of hurting people I love."

"I'm sorry, kid. I tried to – but you don't want to hear that. You want to fight, don't you?" Moreira asked.

"Yes. It's the only thing I want."

"Then let's find your Knockabout a sparring partner."

The door to the org owner's office opened and the owner stood, ready to shake hands with his two o' clock appointment. It confused him to see Olivier wearing his trunks, mouthguard, and fingerless gloves, the latter which the fighter lifted to gently touch against the owner's extended fingers.

THE EXPLODED WOMAN

From the moment she first saw the anatomical artist's work, Marceline knew that she loved him. Marceline's love had always kept her in motion; pulling her forward, step by giggling step, right towards a commercial reverie she'd once had in a department store next to the cosmetics counter. She was eleven then, her eyes fixed on a poster of a kiss, the point of contact between the two illustrated mouths painted a lipstick-red eruption. Their messy liquid shine a magnet for her magpie heart.

She hadn't planned to go out that night – she'd had a chemistry exam to study for – but Marceline's roommate Tessa knew someone else who was showing work at the gallery, and was insistent on her company. Marceline had broken up with her girlfriend Olive the week before, and she was in an exceptionally pliant mood. It was easier to put on a dress than pick up a pen or turn on a laptop. Easier to stay in motion than to stay still.

Marceline zipped and applied and smoothed every last line of herself into order, piled into the car they ordered, and split the fee. Tessa kept cracking jokes about underwire bras really being vampires ("I've never met one yet that wasn't out for my blood") and Marceline smiled but couldn't really feel the emotion that usually came attached to the gesture.

When they arrived at the gallery, it was busy. A perfume of beer and sugary vape clouds lingered by the entrance. Marceline and Tessa pushed through the crowd, Tessa breaking away to go hug her friend. They reunified in a blur of chatter and lotioned limbs that Marceline did not bother to break apart. Instead she let herself get distracted by the art; by an artist.

The anatomical artist was standing next to his sole exhibit: a living human heart, beating beneath the clear sheen of a proprietary synthetic compound he was attempting to secure a patent for. He spoke to a group of people ringing him:

"This heart belonged to a woman who died. But even though she died, her heart never has. It still attempts to propel blood through a body that no longer exists. The rest of her remains were cremated."

"Did you know her?"

Everyone turned to look at Marceline, who flushed with sudden warmth. She hadn't meant to interrupt, but the question had tumbled out so naturally.

The anatomical artist also looked at Marceline, but he met her eyes directly. "I loved her."

In that instant, Marceline wanted his words for herself.

WHEN SHE ASKED for his number, he gave her a business card and a slight glance. A detailed anatomical illustration of branching arteries sprouted words on the square of stiff paper. The only real hint of him was his personal phone number, written in ballpoint directly below the card's business information. Marceline studied the fresh ink. His name was Peter Edmond, and she searched for him online the way children used to write out the names of their crushes in notebooks; looking for signs of fate in every letter of his name. He was there in the pixels and vexingly not-there all at once. His website and bio listed his education and prizes and exhibitions, but nothing personal.

He didn't even know her name. But she still had that number of his, ballpoint blue in her wallet.

Marceline couldn't focus very well and failed her chemistry exam. She told herself it was her fault for texting him the question just before she went to class:

"Do you want to go get coffee?"

The question twisted intangibly all around her, inside her, corkscrewing the air and mangling her stomach. She wanted to keep checking her phone, the need like an itch. Hours later, when her phone finally buzzed with his reply, she recoiled lethargically. She blinked; she'd been staring so hard at the screen that the light still burned in her eyes. Her hands trembled as she entered her passcode and brought up his text.

"I don't drink coffee."

Nausea overwhelmed her. She tried to think of a good reply – something light and quick – but couldn't. She stared blankly at the phone.

Another text from him appeared on the screen: "Do you want to be part of something real?"

Her lips parted.

PETER INVITED her to a bar that she'd never heard of, hidden away in a secret part of an old hotel in the heart of Los Angeles. The hotel had the same odor that hung around museums and libraries; an expensive moldering. The wood panels were dark and so well-polished that Marceline could see faint outlines of their bodies moving along the surfaces as Peter ordered drinks.

"Is this hotel haunted?" She asked. He stared at her. "A lot of old hotels in Los Angeles seem to end up haunted," she said.

The anatomical artist smiled, but the expression was merely a minor flex of his lips. "I'm more interested in corporeal matters."

Marceline took a hasty sip of her cocktail, abruptly dry. The alcohol couldn't compete with the blaze of heat fidgeting through her bloodstream.

"I really loved your work at the gallery," she said.

"I really loved her, too."

He watched her flinch, and took a sip of his bourbon. "Her name was Allison Hollister. We met two years ago, in college. We were engaged. More than anything else, she wanted to help me with my career. Her death changed everything."

"She sounds wonderful," Marceline said. "I'm so sorry you lost her."

"I haven't lost her," he said, his expression closed.

"I mean..." Marceline fumbled, "when someone passes away, it's always so hard – "

"Death is relatively easy. It's immortality that's hard."

Marceline stared at the vague, pale reflection of herself in the wood. "I guess," she said.

"You mentioned over the phone that you were studying chemistry," he said, "what else are you studying?"

"Oh, I'm still undecided. Just taking my requisites until I can figure out what I should do."

Peter looked intently at her. "Have you ever worked as a model?"

Marceline laughed. "Me? Oh, no! Besides, don't you have to be super thin to be a model?"

"No. And sometimes thinness can be a disadvantage – it all depends on who you're modeling for."

She smiled crookedly. "Are you asking me to model for you?"

"I might be."

She took another sip of her cocktail. Now she tasted the sweetness of the drink.

S<small>EX WAS EASY</small>; the anatomical artist wanted to examine every part of his new model, and she wanted to expose herself to him. His gaze was her own; he was eager to give it to her. When he looked at her, she looked at herself through his eyes, and found herself thrilling and new. His words tumbled out: she was his muse, his Marceline, his model in clay. His fingers dug into her, pushing, keen to leave fingerprints behind.

She responded, eager to be marked with the evidence of his desire. The alcohol rolled warmly through her system and purged into sticky orgasms. In his arms, she listened to his plans for his next work of art, and trembled.

Even her fear was a kind of pleasure.

H<small>E HANDED</small> her a contract and a pen to sign it with, and the pen was so impressively heavy and cold that she stared at it for a long moment. Then Peter put his hand on her shoulder and gently squeezed. She signed her name, asking him for the date as she wrote it in.

He had her go to her school's healthcare clinic and get a series of tests done. Her fluids did not betray her; she was within the ranges he had anticipated. Peter had special equipment delivered from a professional embalming company in Texas. He mixed powders and liquids together in a glass beaker while he told her how pretty she was going to be, how good this was going to feel. Peter's tongue slid in her mouth as he depressed the plunger in the syringe. The sting of the fluid beneath her skin muddled with the warmth of the kiss.

He told her it was going to hurt a little. He told her he loved her.

"Are you going out with him again?" Tessa asked.

"Yes."

Tessa folded her arms across her chest. "Are you sure you should go out? You don't seem...healthy."

Marceline stuffed a pair of cutoff shorts and lacy underwear into her gym bag. She glanced sidelong at her roommate as she packed. "What do you mean?"

Tessa shrugged. "I don't know. Are you feeling okay? You just keep moving...slow. Like, slower than usual."

"I'm just tired like everybody else. Finals are coming up."

"That's another thing – I haven't seen you in class in forever. Even Olive is worried about you."

"Wow. How is Olive?"

Tessa frowned. "Okay, just change the subject, then. She's fine. Unlike you."

"Tell her I said 'hello'," Marceline said and smiled, zipping up the bags.

He said that his artistic sources of inspiration were Wunderkammer and her love for him. He showed her the scalpels that he was going to use on her, had her hold each one while he took pictures. "This will be a series of prints," he said. When she looked at the pictures he had taken she couldn't recognize herself, but she was beautifully lit.

His vision of her was ambitious: a woman who could reveal every part of herself for public scrutiny. Not a superficial nudity of skin alone, but a true nudity of the living physical form. Several surgeries had to be undertaken in his studio apartment, late at night. He was a member of strange subreddits. He'd watched several instructional videos online. Slice by slice, the skin of her chest was slowly converted into a door. Stainless steel hinges were installed in her ribcage; she had to be completely accessible to the world. Each one of her organs was painstakingly, slowly sealed, smothered with Peter's clear proprietary compound. Marceline wore sunglasses and listened to music on her headphones as he worked, the morphine drip steady as a wide plastic collar prevented her from accidentally catching a peek of his art before he had finished.

She wasn't allowed to peek.

When Marceline had recovered sufficiently from all the work that Peter did on her torso, he moved onto her limbs, and found a clever way to reattach her muscles so that they could be pulled away from her bones and flipped back again with a lever. For her hands he devised something special.

"See how it snaps out when I push this part right here?" Peter showed her the titanium mechanism and Marceline tried to imagine her hands synthesized with it. Naked bones with hovering muscle and fat and skin all in their distinct snaking orbits above her wrists. A cyberpunk highway made of metal and meat.

"It's exploded anatomy," Peter said, and the passion in his voice was thick. "Isn't it amazing?"

"Amazing," Marceline repeated. She requested more morphine and he complied. She thumbed a button and the music swelled to cover the sound of a bone saw.

MARCELINE KNEW that Tessa was right: she had been growing slower. As the surgeries progressed and she became more perfect in Peter's eyes, it was increasingly difficult to move. Her reattached muscles constantly ached, but it wasn't just the pain that slowed her down. The thick clear compound coating her anatomy fought every fleshy stretch and twitch. It was easier to be still. It was easier to be quiet. It was easier to become art.

Art was subjective; maybe she would become something even Olive could love again.

He cleaned up a corner of the studio and lit it starkly, then had her pose for him. At first she smiled, flirting, but he pulled away from the camera in disgust.

"Not like that. What do you think people want to see here?"

She was stunned. Hurt, and a little angry. He took a picture.

"That's better," he said.

THERE WAS A GALLERY SHOWING. Pictures that Peter had taken of Marceline's naked body, posed with and without scalpels, covered the walls; he didn't have to share space with another artist this time. The event had been wildly hyped. The press was thick in the unusually dense crowd of art-goers.

"I'd like you all to meet possibly the most valuable piece of scientific art in history," Peter said, "may I present my latest work, 'The Exploded Woman'."

Marceline mounted the narrow platform. The applause was enthusiastic. She tossed aside the long white cape she wore – she'd never worn a cape before – and waited, letting the audience take in the edges of the doors embossing the leather of her skin. Cameras flashed and phones were held up to record her.

Her body moved with the smoothness of Peter's insistent rehearsals. She opened up the primary door of her torso. There were gasps, and camera flashes stuttered like lightning. She gestured to her intestines, and then swung them aside using a concealed hinge. Peter leaned forward to open a second, smaller door into her uterus. The murmurs of the crowd increased in volume: he'd left a little sculpture of a fetus inside of Marceline's womb, which he now removed and held above his head, then discarded into the crowd with a wet flick of his wrist. The gathered people shriek-gasped at this audacity. Marceline's ribcage was opened next, her lungs lifted up, her heart exposed to the throng of people that studied her raptly. Everything about her gleamed, red and shiny and full of love. Marceline felt the eyes of the crowd upon her, but Olive wasn't there so she kept looking at Peter and smiling, smiling.

Peter, fondling her liver, kept looking at the crowd.

"IT'S THE NEXT LOGICAL STEP," he said.

"No. I don't want to do it."

"What?"

It was the first time that she had ever defied him.

"I don't want to," she insisted. "Isn't it enough? They're giving you plenty of money to continue your work – "

"Of course they are! Do you think they're fools?" He was

shiny with the expensive bourbon he'd bought to celebrate with.

"Peter, I'm not saying that."

He swept up to her side, spinning her around in a circle before putting her down again and kissing her on the mouth.

"What were you saying?" He grinned at her.

"Peter..." she sighed.

"I love you, Marceline," he said.

"I love you, too," she said, "I just don't want to do this."

He broke away, his sudden absence a rush of cold air. "Let's talk about this tomorrow," he said.

"The answer is going to be the same tomorrow."

Marceline tried to remember the last time she had gone to a class. The last time she had been a student of anything.

HE KEPT ASKING her to let him perform the brain surgery. Why was this one any different? But she couldn't stand the thought of him installing the hinges and proposed titanium mechanisms inside her skull, face, and eye sockets, let alone rummaging inside of her brain.

Where Olive was, still. For now.

"People already love The Exploded Woman, even without doing additional work on her," Marceline said.

"I think the artist who created The Exploded Woman should be trusted to complete his vision," Peter replied lightly.

Marceline's resistance to Peter was new, and she thought for a long, strange minute that he might hit her, the way he looked at her, but then the moment passed and the conversation ended. Peter made dinner that night, which Marceline appreciated as a kind of sideways apology. The risotto's texture was perfect.

"Thank you for making dinner," she said.

He nodded, but didn't reply.

Marceline knew that something was wrong when she woke up in the hospital bed that Peter used for surgeries, not the queen bed that they'd shared for the past few months. Her head ached, throbbing in time to her pulse. Blood and chemicals coated her tongue.

She tried to sit up, but a restraining strap had been tied across her chest. Her head was too light – lighter than usual – and her scalp itched from the fresh shearing it had received.

"You did it. You did the surgery I asked you not to do," she said. Her voice croaked with lingering anesthesia.

"I had to," Peter said. He stood by the door, something pink and wet in his hands. Marceline closed her eyes and kept them pressed tight for a long time, the orbs beneath the skin of her eyelids roving, searching, searching within her own shadows, the motion quick and frantic – then her brow relaxed and she opened her eyes again. She smiled.

"Peter, your work means so much to me. You're now the only person in the world who's seen inside my mind. That's incredible."

He nodded. "I'm glad that you finally seem to understand. You're going to be the most profound piece I have ever created; we're going to be immortals, Marceline. You and I."

"Kiss me, Peter. Celebrate this with me."

In a corner of the room, the heart of Allison Hollister beat on a pedestal. Marceline stared at it for a long moment before she thrust her right hand into the center of the anatomical artist's chest and pulled the secret lever on the titanium exploding mechanism in her wrist.

MARCELINE WALKED DOWN THE STREET, her pulse quick and loud in her ears, carrying nothing from the apartment but a cell phone with Olive's number in it and Peter's heart, wedged alongside her own.

HOSTILE ARCHITECTURE

They just couldn't get enough sleep. They were always on their feet, walking. Until Ever's discount shoes were just strips of rubber. Their legs bundled wires. Their feet all raw blister. The city had gone vertical practically overnight. Not the buildings – Los Angeles couldn't be bothered to build upwards outside of the Downtown area – but everything else. All of the park bench seats were vertical now. The bus stop benches had developed an uncomfortable lean. And what couldn't be made vertical was punctured with enough spikes to make an iron maiden blush. The spikes were everywhere: on the gratings, on ground floor windowsills in skinny strips, tactfully concealed as little brass circles in store doorways by day and up like wardens at night. Lumpy boulders had replaced flat public patches of lawn, and every flat place was policed. If there weren't security guards around ready to move them on, there were the cops. And the cops were always eager to sweep the tent camps on the sidewalks, hassle the folks sleeping there, detain them and throw their possessions away – medications, licenses, bedding – because everything on the sidewalk was garbage to these city employees who'd vowed to keep the streets clean.

But they weren't garbage. They were people: angry, exhausted, restless people. People who couldn't sleep, who weren't being allowed to sleep.

Sleep deprivation does funny things to the mind. It intensifies things. Draws pictures in the gaps of information that start to occur as the brain randomly turns off and on again. Off, and on again.

A September night in Los Angeles: copper light on low clouds.

Off.

Standing in front of a trash can fire behind the long-closed diner, Ever had a vision. An ecstasy. Things unfolded and kept unfolding. First fluffy pages of tissue paper and unwanted mailers curling, charring, then the edges of the graffitied walls. The holes in between the chain-link fence. The light of distant stars smeared by smog. An angel formed within the flames, a thousand mouths smiling. Sparks wept from her lone eye. She extended her endlessly long arms towards them and caressed the topmost curve of their left cheek. Ever could smell the downy fuzz there burn away at her touch.

Her mouths were whispering, but they were talking all at once, and Ever was having difficulty understanding. They wanted to understand. They wanted to know.

"Please," Ever said, "I don't know what you're saying. Tell me so I can understand."

The mouths went silent into smiles, then began again, in unison this time:

Wield.

AND ON AGAIN.

Ever stood in front of a YIELD sign posted next to a freeway on-ramp. It was late, and cold. They were alone. Not even a rat in the weeds. Ever shivered, then reached for a permanent marker that they kept in their coat pocket, uncapped it, and changed "YIELD" to "WIELD" with two quick marks. They stared at their edit. Pocketed their pen.

On top of the WIELD sign a strip of long spikes was affixed; even the birds in the city were denied rest. The spikes were awkwardly attached, half-falling from the top of the sign already even though they looked relatively new. Ever reached up and touched the very tip of one of the thin, nail-like spikes and flinched at its sharpness. Then they reached for the base, the metallic strip part, and pulled a little – it was loose. Slowly Ever peeled the strip free from the sign, careful not to cut themselves. When they were done, they held the weaponized metal ribbon tautly before them. A distant traffic light changed and spilled some red on the spikes.

The tips of the spikes danced, moving with the tremor of Ever's hands. They had never been able to stand the sight of blood. The thought of pain.

THEY TRIED TO SLEEP.

They found a rare clear pocket under a freeway – sheltered from the weather and prying eyes alike. Unclaimed and dry. Ever could hardly believe their luck. They sat down, their back against the wall, knees up to their chest, hands in their coat pockets. They tried to ignore the piercing cold shooting up through the bottom of their jeans from the asphalt. It wasn't too hard; they were tired enough.

Off.

Darkness and flames. The fires drifted, twisting with hypnotic softness, becoming her again. The angel. Sparks wept from her eye. They blushed. A sudden and intense desire seized them – they wanted to kiss the face of the burning angel whose infinite lips parted to whisper, once more:

Wield.

A cop was there.

For no real reason so far as Ever could tell, a cop was just suddenly standing in the middle of their erotic dream. They couldn't understand what he was saying. His words were over-lapping, garbled. It sounded like they were coming from very far away. And then he reached down to touch them.

Ever whipped their right fist straight up into the cop's gut, not removing it from their coat pocket.

Ever laughed. Whipped cream was inexplicably spilling out of the cop's stomach, soaking into their coat and getting their fist sticky. The cop was making funny faces. They removed their fist from their pocket and saw part of the spike strip wrapped around it, pointy part outwards, covered with sugary white goop.

Ever shoved the goopy fist into the cop's face, and he stopped making funny faces, which was good because they were grossing Ever out.

And on again.

Blood everywhere. Flashing red and blue lights. Ever screamed.

Off.

They fell.

It was dark and their legs suddenly couldn't support them so they fell. Their head banged against the pavement. Their bottom teeth pierced their tongue and they recoiled against the fresh blood abruptly filling their mouth, then the back of their throat. They were choking on it.

Another cop came out of the car. He had a gun pointed at them.

Ever was there. Ever wasn't there. Ever was choking on blood. The cop came close, reached out to touch them.

Now Ever's left fist came up and connected with this

cop's gut and his gun went off – too close to Ever's head – but the shot whined wide into the wall. And Ever's left fist kept connecting. And connecting. And connecting. Because their dream had turned nightmare and there was a body on top of them that they did not want and it kept moving, it kept moving and should not be moving at all. Their left hand was wet. Warm. They gripped the other half of the spike strip so tightly that the edges of the ribbon cut into their palm. When the body finally went still and Ever could hear things again they heard a chime, a note so lyrical and pure that it could have been the voice of an angel singing in Ever's ears.

They shoved the cop's body off of them and stood, spitting out blood, looking for her. Only the red and blue lights were there. The two bodies on the ground. The distant song of a siren.

Ever followed the torch song.

DAWN DESATURATED THE NIGHT.

A project: a real divine DIY. Ever was preoccupied with it; inspiration was truly everywhere. Ever wandered by a pile of abandoned furniture heaped up on the curb. A mattress had been left out overnight and the dew that had collected there was steaming off in a funk that Ever could visibly see, and therefore steered clear of. Next to the mattress was the broken iron frame of a bed, partially disassembled and jutting out awkwardly into the street.

Ever walked over to the iron frame and pulled one of the long, unbent bars free. Bounced it in their hands. Hefted it up in the air experimentally.

A security door rattled. Someone exited from a nearby apartment. Ever was already walking away with the iron bar held close to their body, their heart pounding too loud for their liking, their calves screaming for them.

THE DAY HAD DEVELOPED A FLICKER.

The flicker wasn't always there, only sometimes. A little shadow lurking in the middle of the light. A dark rim around people like an outline or an aura. Electricity was louder. Their knuckles kept creeping up to insulate their ears from the constant buzz that leaked from light sockets and hummed in the power lines.

They just couldn't get enough sleep. They tried to buy a cup of coffee and sit down at a fast food place that usually let Ever in but the cashier, Joan, said that her boss was watching today. New policy: you had to buy food to sit down at the tables. Ever understood perfectly. They ordered their coffee to go. They wanted to laugh; they couldn't, but they wanted to. Joan kept looking at them funny.

The caffeine did nothing. Like pouring water into the sea. Ever drank it down to the dregs. Kept walking. Kept listening to that song they couldn't quite make out. Followed it up and down the long blocks of Los Angeles.

Kept ducking into alleys to work on their craft project.

A DISTANT ROAR, soft cheering and applause rebounded along the asphalt and concrete. Ever blinked at the echoes. It sounded like a speaker system. Muffled booming words were punctuated with more applause. Were they all witnessing the angel's glory? They hugged their craft project to their chest and followed the sounds, found a big crowd. Hovered at the edge of it.

A politician was speaking. Some recently elected mayor or governor in an expensive brown suit. Flashes went off from the gaggle of professional and amateur photographers in the crowd gathered around him.

"We're working hard to keep the homeless off of our streets. To protect our hard-working, tax-paying families from being exposed to – "

That was one voice. The politician's voice. But Ever heard another voice singing through the sound system, speaking from multiple mouths. A holy voice. They just had to get closer to hear it better. To understand.

Ever looked around. The speakers were mounted on top of flat truck beds. They picked one of the trucks and started heading towards it, pushing through the throngs of people. At first it was difficult, but once people started to notice the blood-stains they gave them more room. When they reached the truck, however, they encountered some resistance.

A security guard leaned against the truck, his gym-puffed muscles folded across his chest.

"Where do you think you're going?"

Ever blinked at him. Took a step towards the truck bed. The guard unfolded his arms and shoved against the center of Ever's chest.

Ever launched their craft project up from its hiding place by their left armpit and a long iron javelin scraped to a fine stabbing point pierced the underside of the guard's jaw and exited the top of his skull. Just the tip of the javelin jutted up, like the tiniest black bird beak in a nest of crushed brain and hair. Ever regretted that they had nothing to feed it.

Other people were shouting, raising phones, standing back. They were just more voices to ignore in a sea of noise. Ever removed the holy javelin from the guard's head and mounted the truck bed. Pressed their head against the speakers' foam to catch the buzzing, whispering, crackling voices leaking from them.

"I'm listening," Ever said. "I want to understand."

"An eyesore that lowers the property values of our homes –" said the speaker.

And the angel's voice, there but undiscernible, buried beneath so much sound.

Ever trembled. The people standing closest to the truck were making strange faces. They hefted their holy javelin and stared at the politician, whose useless words kept getting in the way. They thought they might be close enough now to be understood.

Heat surged through Ever, elevating their spine, bracing their arms. Sparks wept from the pores on their forearms, singeing the hair. They were smoking, blazing, launching their iron javelin through the air on a sacred flight that ended spiking the politician right through the middle, pinning him backwards to the earth. Bright confetti fistfuls of his blood were everywhere. Ever laughed and laughed because the blood kept changing color like a beautiful party trick.

THE EDGES of the world were curling, burning. Ever saw angels standing in the crowd, their clothing worn out, their eyes undying flames. In between the screaming, panicked people, the divine were watching. Waiting for their chance to catch fire.

And on and on again.

PIPELINE BOY

"I'm not like them,' Andi said, fumbling for the words like the teenaged boy halfway up her shirt. The callus on Grant's left thumb persistently circled a mole he had mistaken for a nipple. Everything was uncomfortably imprecise. Adolescently incorrect. "I mean I have breasts and the other parts, I guess, I'm just...not a girl inside," she said.

"Uh huh," Grant said, pinching the meat along her ribs with his grip. She winced, and guided his hands back up to her breasts, which could take more punishment.

"I just don't get other women. You know what I mean? We never seem to have much in common," she said.

"Sure," he said.

"Are you listening?"

"Yeah," he mumbled, his mouth full of flesh.

"What do you think?"

He shrugged, the hump of his shoulder bumped her left thigh.

"Do you like me?" Andi asked.

In reply to that he unbuckled and slid his belt free from his jeans. Andi could still smell the bright burn of gasoline on his denim from when he'd refueled her car earlier, his carelessness with the pump handle a kind of callousness she'd wanted on her body, then. The smell of danger.

Did she still? She asked the question with a limp kiss, a timid grope of his erection.

The subsequent sex was like this: a series of blatant misunderstandings. Questions of stumbling breathless curiosity answered in monosyllable. A projection of his fantasies onto her body like a movie only he was allowed to watch. Hollow-eyed, panting to match his private pornographic pantomime, Grant persevered. He continued. When Andi asked to see, to know what drove him on so unsynchronized from her moans and motions he told her now she'd made him soft, it was her fucking fault, fuck! It was Andi's fault that he couldn't finish. It was her fault the sex wasn't any good. He was going on and on about it in the bathroom, a long tirade that Andi didn't have the energy to care about. Not really. Because right now she was trying to figure out why she felt like a stranger in the woods of her body grown wilder by her recent actions.

She pressed her fingers against the smoothness of her own skin, a slippery slickness that never gave her comfort. Even unshaved her legs and arms never grew enough hair for her own liking. She wanted it dense. Thick like wild underbrush or the fur of a woodland creature. Not like other girls with their civilized skin regimens and creams. Not like Jenny Alvarez, money-cuddled in coordinated skirts and sweaters, cashmere cupping her smooth flesh like kisses, softly smiling at the jokes Andi spent all of algebra class coming up with. Yes, smiling at her. Smiling at Andi.

Andi moaned, a sound escaping, and Grant looked at her with new interest. Dick in hand he asked if he could try again and she said yes, and in that moment as they gazed off into the horizons of their own private fantasies the flare of their projection lights intersected, briefly; the consequent dazzle felt like love, or at least a part of it, that overwhelming giddy lifting, sudden and intense, but it should have felt like a klaxon call –

something inescapable and screaming stop. Something wiser. Something warning her away.

Andi wanted to be chosen; selected not for her outstanding qualities but because she sensed that if she was chosen, she would know she was meant to be the way she was inside. She was designed to be this boyish bravado, cocky and laughing, this clumsy fortitude stumbling forward, tripping really but unable to catch himself. He doesn't realize yet that he has to fall. To bruise his knees on concrete. Before Andi knows what to do next the trans boy has to reach his own velocity first.

At night in Grant's bed, cocooned in sheets that smelled like nineteen-year-old cis boy and gasoline and booze, Andi had the nightmare again.

He knew what sleep paralysis was: he'd read the online literature about the man with the hat and all that crap. He knew.

But his dream was always a little different from those.

They inevitably started in the dark. He closed his eyes and Grant's bedroom dimmed into a sudden obscurity so quickly and absolute that only Andi remained visible, lit by an unknown fae brightness. This light revealed that the bed Andi rested upon was actually an altar, the base carved white marble, slightly elevated above a sea of cheap plastic chairs. The kind of chairs usually found in schools and government waiting rooms. People were seated in those chairs. Or not people, maybe, but things like people. They shifted, restless, in the darkness. Their eyes glittered.

The light and the marble made Andi their offering; a sacrifice. Andi was afraid. Andi was ecstatic. He trembled beneath the approach of a faceless priest in long gray robes who extended a hand to take a piece of him. The fingers reached for Andi and kept reaching. Grant, passed out and dreaming something new, might as well have been a million miles away instead of a few inches. His pale blonde eyebrows moved in sleep like wind-lifted weeds.

Someone must be picked.

Andi woke up, his heart heavy and quick, knowing with absolute certainty that he had until Sunday – a month away – and then the choice would be made. The priest would take.

ANDI COULDN'T TELL HIM. He couldn't tell Grant that he was trans, for starters, because he'd only just started dating him and Andi felt like he had to protect the fact of his gender, watch over it carefully just now in its tender infancy. He couldn't tell if Grant was worthy of knowing this profound truth: who Andi really was. It was a mystery.

There was also the romance of the decision, the private sacrifice. The beauty of giving so much. And Andi had always wanted to be picked. It was his favorite thing.

Didn't the priest want him, *Andi*, specifically? He remembered the hand, fingers long like twigs reaching for him. There was so much desire there. So much yearning.

Indecisive Andi daydreamed through the good times: dates doodled over his days with Grant like cartoon hearts. Aspirations at forever were performed in front of parents.

"I'm not like other girls –" Andi tried to explain, again.

"Shut up," Grant said, again.

AT NIGHT THE PRIEST RETURNED. Andi woke to find him incubus-like perched atop his ribcage, leering over him, mouthless and quiet. His long fingers twitched against the door of Andi's chest, a gentle query that made the young trans man shudder in revulsion and ecstasy.

Someone must be picked.

WAS Grant worthy of Andi's sacrifice? That was the question. Grant was a game of love-me-not: Grant was so kind; Grant was so unkind. The difference depended upon the number of petals plucked that day, or some other equally random and unpredictable factor. As far as Andi could tell he had no discernable impact on the outcome, not really. It was the weather or whether Grant loved him or not.

Mid-month, abruptly: more days started ending in love-me-not than love-me.

In this climate of unlove, Andi found it difficult to advocate for his own passions, large and small. He reduced. He cut. He went without. He malnourished. He was failing most of his classes at the community college he attended. He could agree to nothing but going along with whatever Grant planned for them – asking for anything else was unthinkable. A sin.

The revelation came in Andi's retraction – a snail-like folding into himself. A minimizing of his soul that took too much. He ignored Jenny Alvarez's repeated invitations to cozy study sessions, like the ones they'd shared at the beginning of the semester before things went to shit. Instead he stayed at home, which meant he stayed in one small corner of Grant's apartment. Like the increasing density of a collapsing star, everything was drawn into one point, firm. A distinct shape: Andi's own. There was nothing else. Denying his existence was no longer possible. He had something he wanted to fight for – himself. He'd been asking the wrong question: it wasn't about whether Grant was worthy or not, it was whether Andi deserved to be saved.

He always had been.

$$\mathcal{P}_x \, {}^\circ_\circ$$

AT NIGHT in Grant's bed Andi fought the pull of sleep. Grant was on his phone, skimming through memes and videos. He still didn't know. Perhaps he should.

"Grant, I wanted you to know something," Andi said.

"Hm?"

"I'm trans. A man. I'm a trans man."

"What?"

Grant was off his phone now. Attentive.

Andi swallowed, looking for safety. "I'm a trans man," he repeated.

There was none given. A roar like drowning.

$$\mathcal{P}_x \, {}^\circ_\circ$$

SLEEP PULLED Andi down into dreaming like a drug – one swift narcotic tug under. It was better being unconscious because it was better not being there. Andi's face hurt from crying. He wanted to forget the ache under his skin. There were a lot of things he wanted to forget.

In dreams the darkness went on like a light; the fae spot stark above him. And Grant. Grant was there, too.

Above them both loomed the long-robed priest, his hand for the first time positioned between the two of them equidistant: posed as a question, or a choice. Waiting.

"Pick him," Andi said.

The priest flickered, his spine creasing into a nod briefly

before his gray hand descended, fingers long then longer yet, impossibly so and crunching directly into the center of Grant's chest. Grant's eyes were open during wet impact. A scream gargled out, his blue eyes locked with Andi's own.

Andi didn't look away. Not even when the priest started moving around inside of Grant's ribcage and pulling at things. Not even when blood ruptured like sewage from a city pipe out of Grant's sinuses. It made him sick to look and hear, but Andi wanted to bear witness. He wanted to know all of it.

"Who will you take next?" the trans man asked the priest when he was finally done.

The gray fingers twitched at the question. The seconds went long between them.

"Who?" Andi asked again.

"The one who comes next," the priest said. His voice was rusty from disuse, a harmonium of surprise hidden under his gray hood.

"Who will come next?" Andi persisted.

"Someone," the priest said, "someone must be picked."

"I'm not like other girls...because I'm not a girl," Andi said, the smile on his face warm with the truth of it, a little embarrassed but honest all the same. A lot had changed since he had decided to start medical transition. A few hairs had even sprouted on the underside of Andi's chin; the early attendees of a goatee.

"Sounds like another pick me to trans masc pipeline," they joked. Serenity always smelled like sandalwood and rosemary, like a pot of soup or a hearth, like comfort was within reach. Jenny Alvarez hadn't been interested in Andi once he'd started transitioning, but Serenity was much more than interested. Andi's fingers found their hips and pulled them to meet his own automatically. They groaned, a gentle sound.

"What do you want?" Andi asked them.

"Everything. Please."

The subsequent sex was like this: a series of fiery questions, unquenchable by simple answers, becoming complex wildfires burning trees into self-immolating orgasms whole mountainsides scorched raw into submission. He sucked them off to the rhythm of their limbic system, to arcane bloodstream music only he could hear. As they climaxed beneath him Andi wedged his t dick into the crevice of their ass and rode them both ragged into wet surrender. They invented and investigated both their mysteries and shared familiarities, cosmic and questionable, because Andi loved Serenity so very deeply. He would do anything for them.

Yes, he would.

ANDI HAD ALWAYS WANTED to be picked. In sleep he waited for the priest to come. He didn't have to wait long.

"Pick me," Andi grinned into the darkness. He squeezed his fist until his knuckles looked like the zigzag of teeth. Like he was hungry. Like his opponent might not be the one winning after all.

THE PERSISTENT DRIP FROM 203

THEY FROWNED AT THE EAST WALL OF THEIR APARTMENT, which kept twitching. Ferris wondered if they should call the Dermatologists. It was hard to get hold of them, especially during a seasonal change. Winter caused a whole mess of issues with moisture regulation and peeling. But the coat of lotion that Ferris had applied earlier that week was still fresh, and there wasn't anything obvious for them to peel, search as they might.

Ferris picked up the stiff bristle broom that they kept by the compost bin and approached the twitchy wall. They turned the broom bristle-end up, and vigorously rubbed against the vertical surface. The wall's grayish skin flushed carmine from the fresh abrasion. Ferris stopped, removed the broom, and waited.

No more twitching. Just the regular, glacial rock of the wall's deep breathing. Ferris patted the wall as if it were the flank of a horse. "I got your itchy back, Hill," Ferris said. Even though they had no idea if their wall actually composed the Hill's "back".

Scientists refused to disclose the species of the Hill, but in truth it was likely such a slurry of genetic manipulation that any one species wouldn't do. The Hill was alive; a rounded mass of muscle and fat and skin anchored into a smaller rocky hill. Designed to provide a cheaper alternative to most climate control systems, the Hill was comfortably warm in winter, and its sweat ran the cooling system in the summer. Thirteen floors of apartments had been built around the Hill, wreathing the fleshy, faceless mass in neatly engineered layers of polyconcrete. There were singles, two-bedroom units, and even a few three-bedroom units all outfitted with stylish contemporary amenities. Planters decorated the edges of the buildings, packed to abundance with local greenery. With its elaborate girdle of flexible girders and walls the Hill itself was invisible from the outside, merely implied as the apartments gently rocked with its soft, steady breathing.

The residents had been carefully selected by a marketing team chosen by the investors. Ferris was a tattoo artist paid by the Hill team to do mural work. The residents were regularly exposed to the Hill's naked flesh, but only in wall-sized patches in their apartments and out in the halls, laundry rooms, and lounges. The shared public spaces were slowly filling with Ferris's work: landscapes, mostly. Deserts studded with Joshua trees. Seaside vistas. Lush gardens. An occasional starlit night, the constellations accurate and inked with a pigment that glowed greenly in the dark. Some of the other residents would watch Ferris as they worked and stop to observe, then ask them to do a piece on their walls. Mostly landscapes or fake windows looking out onto other landscapes. Ferris knew what they were worth and got a decent amount of work at the Hill. They also had to explain that portraits and figures weren't their strength a lot. They liked horizons. Perspective.

Ferris's living room and bedroom were along the east wall. At first it had been unnerving, trying to live and sleep alongside this giant, unknowable being. But after a while Ferris had grown to enjoy Hill's company (their unofficial name for the "biological innovation" that the Hill team stressed residents to NOT familiarize with and NOT name) and even developed an affection for the big lug.

Ferris went to the cabinets under their kitchen sink and removed a plastic tub of lotion and a rag. They dabbed the rag into the lotion and applied a bit to the reddish patch of wall that they'd made.

They hadn't tattooed their own walls yet. Six months had come and gone and Ferris still couldn't decide what to do. Their digital sketchbook was straining for memory beneath the plurality of their files, but still, they left their apartment walls blank. They accepted the wait; very good ideas sometimes took Ferris a very long time. But at the same time, the blank walls made them restless, impatient.

Ferris put the lotion and rag back under the sink. Hopped into the shower. As the warm water came down they stretched out their arms and looked at the long tangles of cityscapes and leafing branches tattooed there. The colors weren't fading too badly, and the lines were still fairly distinct.

Ferris hugged themself, skyscrapers and greenery wreathing their heart, certain that inspiration would come.

In the middle of the night, the drip returned.

Ferris sat up, swallowing acid that had crept up the back of their throat mid-dream. Half-remembered sketches of arteries bending like architecture flooded their mind's eye. They blinked the visions away. The drip was loud, echoing in the confines of their polyconcrete bedroom. They pushed aside their quilt and put on a pair of slippers. They checked the bathroom plumbing – the taps and pipes beneath the sink – dry as old bones. Checked the sink in the kitchen – cluttered with dinner's dishes but dry. Checked the hydroponics that fed the planters – no punctures, no audible drips found there.

They went back to their bedroom and stared up at the ceiling.

The drip was loudest in there. Persistent. A flat, wet dripping like rain hitting wood. Which was impossible because the ceiling wasn't made of wood, just more polyconcrete, and besides a tenant lived above Ferris – the 203 to Ferris's 103.

Ferris had sent a complaint about the dripping sound in to the Dermatologists before. The infamously hard-to-reach professionals had even come by a couple months ago to inspect. After they were interviewed, Ferris had hung around as unobtrusively as they could manage while the Dermatologists examined their ceiling and knocked on 203's door. It turned out that the tenant in 203 was also a Dermatologist, a high-salaried doctor. She'd answered the Dermatologists' questions in a tone of voice that betrayed nothing except perhaps some highly understandable fatigue: Dermatologists worked long hours and had a range of intense tasks to oversee and perform at the Hill apartments. Most of them were tired in their off hours.

She said she hadn't heard the drip.

"Might be something in the cooling system," one of the Dermatologists had said to Ferris, her beige rubber suit squeaking in addendum.

"Like what?" they'd asked.

The Dermatologist had given a shrug-squeak. "Some kind of fluids. Sweat. Water. Sebum. You don't want to know. It gets gross. Skin stuff!"

"Isn't that bad?"

Another shrug-squeak. "It depends. If a pore gets backed up to the point that it's going to rupture the polyconcrete, you can bet we'll have to drain it. And that can be a big procedure. But don't worry, you're lucky! You live right below a Dermatologist. If there's an emergency, Dr. Richards is trained to handle it," she had said. Then she'd given a squeaky sign off as she'd waved goodbye to them in the hall.

Ferris sat on their bed and stared up at the dripping sound. No team of Dermatologists were there tonight, and even if they called for them, who knows if it would still be audibly dripping when the doctors showed up? It hadn't been the last time.

As Ferris stared, they thought they saw the slightest twitch at the very top of their east wall. They frowned. Turned on a light by the bed. Focused their attention on the topmost part of the east wall. Waited. Listened to the steady, persistent drip.

Another twitch – quick but pronounced – then nothing.

They went and got the stiff bristle broom from its place in the kitchen, and proceeded to scratch the twitchy patch of skin by the ceiling.

At the first touch of the broom, the entire wall crumpled, flushing a deep purple color that Ferris had never seen Hill turn before and trembling so hard that Ferris's collection of ceramic cats shook. Ferris jerked the broom away and the wall relaxed – but slowly. Begrudgingly. Pore by pore. But Hill kept twitching, even after relaxing back to its usual flat desaturated beige. And Ferris noticed a deep yellow-green tint by the ceiling that they hadn't seen before.

They put the broom away and tried to go back to sleep. The drip kept going, dripping on and on through their dreams. The drip became a musical note. A bird call. A voice they could almost make out if they just listened carefully enough.

THE DRIP WAS BLOOD.

A drop of salty blood fell into their open mouth below as they screamed awake. Directly above them a rusty-red circle dotted the ceiling of their bedroom. Tasting iron, they thought about their mother for the first time in a very long time.

They spat a bubbly red blob onto the floor, fumbled for their phone, and left a blurry, quick message on the Dermatology emergency line because all of the available operators were busy at ten in the morning. They ran to the sink and washed the blood out of their mouth. Scrubbed their face against a towel.

Found an empty sauce pot in the kitchen and placed it underneath the drip. Waited for the Dermatologists to arrive.

THEY HAD to empty the pot. Once. Twice. Four times. Called the Dermatologists and left some more messages. Kept calling. Kept leaving messages. The spot on the ceiling grew larger. Wider. They dumped the pot out again. Had a craving to vape even though they had quit three years ago. They put on music, something sugary and light. Then they turned it off again because they couldn't stand the sugary lightness. They made dinner but didn't have the appetite to eat it, and finally threw their eggplant and rice into the compost bin.

The night was bad. The next day was worse.

The sauce pan had overflowed in the night, drenching the bed in warm blood. Ferris had to unpeel themselves from their congealed, scabbing sheets. Stop hyperventilating. Take a shower and get themselves steady again. Ferris checked their phone for messages – nothing but a reminder about a mural gig tomorrow. They called the Dermatologists. Left another message. Called every contact they could think of on the Hill team and left messages for good measure. Nobody picked up. Nobody returned their calls.

Around noon, another spot started bleeding a few feet away from the first spot. The east wall was constantly twitching now, rattling the ceramic cats into persistent faint peals. A geneticist had told Ferris once that the Hill couldn't make any sounds because it didn't have vocal cords. Hill couldn't moan or cry.

Ferris made a decision; they were going to meet their upstairs neighbor.

THEIR HEART RACED. They knew this was a bad idea. But still Ferris stood there, and knocked on the door of 203. They waited. They could hear someone moving inside, approaching the door. They wiped the sweat on their palms along their pants, quickly.

Dr. Richards opened the door and almost immediately shut it again, but Ferris jammed a rubber and steel-wrapped toe in the way. The doctor's door caught on their boot and remained open. Dr. Richards stared at them. Ferris smiled, their eyes more than a little wild.

Ferris's tattoo machine was something special.

A person couldn't tattoo the Hill with a regular tattoo machine – at least not very effectively. Before moving to the Hill, Ferris had been known for designing and building unusual tattoo machines for unique circumstances: under-water machines, steam-powered machines, even a nano machine that could be aimed inside of an artery. So Ferris had designed a custom machine to do the jobs at the Hill, with refillable cannisters of ink the size of fire extinguisher cans and the smallest gauge needle as wide across as a thumb knuckle.

"Step back from the door," Ferris said. "You're going to

show me the east wall of your bedroom, and if everything's hunky-dunky, I'm going to leave you alone. That's all. Sound good?"

"And if I refuse?" he asked.

"Then we're going to find out what your body does with two liters of iron oxide black."

"You're being completely unreasonable. I make more in a year than you do in a decade – you shouldn't even be allowed to live in this property. I'm going to file a complaint with the Hill team," he said. "You *will* face punishment."

Ferris nodded. "I might. Let's find out."

Dr. Richards opened the door and stepped back from it, his hands raised. Ferris waved the needle of the machine at him. "Lead the way," they said.

They really hoped that Dr. Richards wouldn't notice that the machine needed to be plugged in to be operational.

The east wall of the living room looked fine – the same grayish skin that came standard in most of the apartments – but when they crossed the threshold into the bedroom, Ferris had to suppress a wave of nausea that rose up in them.

Dr. Richards had cut into the side of Hill so deeply that an inch of blood coated the floor. Lights and plastic tarps were everywhere, a camera on a tripod was aimed at the broad incision.

"What the hell are you doing to poor Hill?" Ferris said.

"You're just an ignorant nothing. A citizen. What do you know about anything? The team pulled the budget on my experiments – not because they couldn't stomach my work, oh no, but because the company had a 'change in their projected brand image'. What the hell does that even mean? My studies on the purpose of pain in living architecture are far more important than some popularity contest!"

Ferris had to keep looking at Dr. Richards or else they were going to vomit. They stared at him. "You hurt Hill on purpose?"

"Of course I did. My reputation depends on this raw data," he said. Ferris realized that they couldn't see his hands.

"Raise your hands," they said.

He did, a heavy-duty scalpel the size of a bread knife elevating in his right fist, then angling down abruptly at Ferris's face.

Ferris thrust the tattoo machine forward while shoving themself back to hit the polyconcrete wall behind them, hard. As their back teeth clicked together the needle sank into the center of Dr. Richards, puncturing his chest. He slashed Ferris's left arm, bisecting a skyscraper. Blood was everywhere, and Ferris found themself shoving hard, harder, then slipping in blood as they dropped the machine and ran, skidding, into the living room. They panted, waiting for pursuit, clinging to the fresh cut on their arm.

But no pursuit came. Their aim had pierced true, and Dr. Richards was dead.

203 HAD A BATHTUB. Ferris filled the bathtub up with warm water. Added all the salt that they could find, stirred it into a mixture with their fist, then filled a plastic bucket they found nearby with the salt water mixture, walked it over to the bloody gap in the wall, and threw it in.

The wall twitched, but only a little. Ferris went back to the bathtub, then returned with more salt water to flush out Hill's wound. Again. Again. They washed the damaged flesh until Hill stopped flinching. Until the east wall stopped twitching, and Hill's breathing was steady and slow again. It reminded them of being young and helpless. Of their dead mother carefully hand picking gravel out of Ferris's knee, once, on a street corner a long time ago. Wound care was something that good tattoo artists excelled at.

Ferris sighed, fanning their neck with the edge of their hand. It was muggier in 203 than it was down in 103, and they still couldn't think of a single thing that they wanted to put on their apartment walls. It felt like the inspiration for this one would be a long time coming.

HUSBAND FOR THE PUMPJACK KING

CONDUIT WAS AN UGLY PILE OF RECTANGLES BAKING IN the California desert: fields of dead things and prefabricated boxes and ancient motel signs half-lit by dying yellow bulbs. A place renowned for its gas station, which was unremarkable. Both the town's motels were missing arbitrary necessities that travelers generally desired: random windows and walls and doorknobs. There was something penitential in the place's design, a self-flagellation forcing the elements to play the flogger.

A vow of discomfort.

On top of the rectangles were the pumpjacks; shiny fleas keeping rhythm as they drank. Oil company logos were tattooed across their metal flanks.

Ambrose pulled into one of the ambiguous spaces in the gas station lot and left the motor of his car running. He could feel the heat of the desert sun blistering through the glass all around him, adding more potentially cancerous spots to his exposed limbs. His sunscreened skin more pink than peach now. He leaned against the firm stream coming from the air conditioning, the collar of his button-up undone, his neck exposed. With his eyes closed the cold air was like a hand on his throat. He was going to grow an Adam's apple there eventually. He'd only just started taking testosterone, but his left hand was still compelled to search for one. His fingertips touched disappointment. Of course there was nothing new there: it had only been four months. Four months was just the beginning of the changes he would experience. When he thought about the things yet to come – more body hair, his deepening voice, even potentially going bald – he felt profoundly steady. Calm. Calmer and yet somehow simultaneously more excited than he'd ever been before.

The calmness, the excitement; two disparate things fighting for space within him at once; the sensation was almost nostalgic. A mild nausea trilling in his gut as his parents fought in front of him. Ambrose had never cared for nostalgia – it made him uneasy – the way a person could get so lost in it that they'd try to make the things in front of them into mawkish ghosts of what wasn't anymore. Or worse, what never had been. He sharply missed Cal and Ivy; his love for his two partners that he'd left back in the city overwhelmed him. Cal's comforting arms. Ivy's steady wisdom. What the hell was he even doing out here, anyway? The trans man was reaching for his phone to send a couple texts home when a shadow fell across his windshield.

It wasn't a person; a crow had landed on top of a short chain-link fence nearby. Ambrose frowned. It looked like the bird had strands of human hair gripped in its beak. They were wispy and curly and blonde, bouncing with every inquisitive jerk of the bird's neck.

He stared at the crow for a moment too long before he remembered his camera, but when he reached for it on the passenger seat the bird took off. Ambrose took the camera out of his tote bag anyway, carefully removing the plastic cap from the Zeiss lens; he'd be ready for the next shot.

Knuckles banged the metal of the car roof and the sound and the silhouette that came with it nearly made Ambrose drop his expensive camera onto the gear shift, lens-first. A lanky white man wearing coveralls leaned across the driver's side window, his brow distorted by shadows and the curve of the glass that he pressed against. A name was stitched into his front pocket, stained and thread-plucked to illegibility. His expression was equally difficult to decipher. The man was either smiling or he was not.

"THEY'RE OUT THERE in the desert microdosing crude oil or some shit. Pumpjack cults, they're called," Cal had told him.

"What? You're not for real," Ambrose had replied. He'd been naked and in Cal's arms at the time and he was easily distracted by how good it felt to be in Cal's arms. He'd traced a path through the hair on their forearms out to the thick veins twisting beneath the brown skin on the back of Cal's right hand, coarse to smooth. Cal's mother was white, their father a second-generation immigrant from Brazil; neither of them had supported Cal when they'd come out as non-binary a few years previously.

"I'm not kidding. It was big local news for a while. Ask Ivy," Cal had said.

"I just might when I see her tomorrow!" Ambrose grinned at them.

Cal had nudged him. "I'm serious! I think this could be a good lead. It really works with your style, you know? The cult angle and everything."

"I told you that I'm not covering cults anymore. You know that," Ambrose had replied.

"Yeah, but these aren't *real* cults, that's just what they're called. It's probably just some teenagers shooting up motor oil or something. Tiktok shit. Nothing good, but nothing that'll come after you."

Nothing like what happened in Malibu. Nothing like that tired boy, blood black where his nose had once been, tongue like a stop sign, semen fresh on wet scabs, redly laughing at Ambrose's revulsion tucked behind a camera lens: *"You don't believe in anything."*

"I don't know. I'll think about it," Ambrose had finally said.

THE CIS MAN said Ambrose should call him Al, and then proceeded to stare at him, three feet of cramped, musty air from the gas station's interior tight between them. Sickly humidity vented from an ancient drink refrigerator directly onto Ambrose's ankles. Ambrose was uncomfortable, but accustomed to staring; his appearance did not cleanly indicate "cis man" or "cis woman", and there were a lot of people in California who liked to think cleanly. Rightly. Their brains so scrupulously washed that nothing new was allowed inside lest it spoil the carpet or rearrange the knickknacks.

"I see that there's two motels in town, which one do you recommend?" Ambrose asked.

"Nobody spends the night in Conduit," Al said.

"Then why do they have the motels?"

"Locals, mostly."

"I see," Ambrose said.

Al snorted. "What do you see, exactly?"

Ambrose shrugged. "I don't know, yet. How the motels stay in business, I guess."

"Why do you want to spend the night?"

His intensity was unexpected: Ambrose's heartrate shot up. "This place seems interesting," he replied.

Al made a sound that was almost a laugh. "Nobody says that about Conduit."

"I like the pumpjacks."

At that, Al went back to staring. Ambrose felt hell on his ankles, sweat on his temples. The minutes stretched long. His stomach churned nostalgically. Outside, through the grime of the windows, figures could be discerned: wavering, walking in the heat.

"You want gas?" Al asked.

"Sure, I'll take twenty."

And Ambrose knew that he should leave; go outside, start putting the gas into his car, then maybe put the engine on and steer back onto the freeway, go home. Go back to the comfort of Ivy and Cal. Los Angeles wasn't so far, and there were a couple of new podcasts downloaded onto Ambrose's phone. He didn't have to do this.

"Do you happen to know anything about kids microdosing oil around here?" he found himself asking instead.

$$\mathcal{S}_x \, \overset{o}{\circ}$$

THE BOY WAS NINETEEN, his friends a little older, a little younger. Their genders and ethnicities varied, but their noses were all smashed open into perpetual stigmatas, bleeding wide, the antibiotics and stimulants flowing like water down the Malibu cliffs. There were rumors of a celebrity, white and moldering in a bedroom somewhere, his money funding everything in between his increasingly pitiful orgasms. The boy and his friends were only too happy to show off the celebrity to Ambrose. At one point the boy had puppeted the back of his drowsing, well-known skull, reciting his famous catchphrase and then laughing uproariously. The celebrity was dying in slow motion, and they were his comforting chorus, pure faith upon their faces and holy fire in their loins. For they were the ultimate transcendence of circumstance: crucibles of their painful fates. Finding pleasure in the unpleasurable while pleasuring the unpleasurable. They were strange magicians dancing in rings around bonfires on a private beach, unbothered by neighbors or laws. Making water flow uphill. It was Ambrose who lacked faith, who couldn't find a greater purpose to sustain his own existence. Without Ivy and Cal, who was he? Without his love for them, what did he have to offer?

Gallery after gallery, unpeopled but stuffed full of his photographs of cultists blankly staring back at him. Reviews calling his work trashy and predatory. Puerile. Empty. Like there was a hole in Ambrose, and because of it everyone was able to stare right through him.

"You don't believe in anything."

"Like vegetable oil or massage oil or what?" Al asked, but he didn't want an answer because he was still going. He was quick, now. Al didn't know anything about those kids on the radio microwaving or whatthefuckever, but he knew Sam, who happened to know Thomas, who happened to know Bud, who might know something about a little party at the edge of town, if Ambrose wanted to stick around. The sun set while Ambrose stared at old postcards firmly embedded into a corkboard behind the counter. Smudges like rust ringed the tack heads. He couldn't make out the names of any destinations, only the vague squiggles of horizons. Suggestions of colors.

Ambrose squinted. Were a few strands of fine brown hair pinned in between the paper and cork of a postcard there? He took a step closer to try and see better.

Al's embroidered coveralls abruptly blocked the view. Ambrose looked at him. Al lifted his lips in an expression that wasn't really a smile. "You want to stay in that spot any longer, you're going to have to buy something."

AMBROSE BOUGHT a soda that came in a limited edition can for an Olympic event that had happened over a decade ago.

He stood outside with the can sweating condensation in his hand. At the edges of empty architectural boxes people lingered, vanished. Ambrose discreetly aimed his camera lens at these distant figures and took pictures. He kept doing it while he walked to the car, then moved the vehicle to a pump and refueled. Kept at it while he drank from the anachronistically Olympian can. When he zoomed into the pictures he saw young people – kids in their late teens or early twenties – wearing shirts or shorts or pants that were all lightly dusted with the desert. Nothing unusual. There was nothing mysterious about their vanishing, either: the kids were walking behind buildings and the heat rippled the light like thick glass. These were just some kids, a little dirty and trying to stay out of sight. Away from adults, and who could blame them?

Ambrose took another picture, zoomed in again, and froze. This time a teenager stared directly back at the camera. The gaze was uncomfortably familiar.

Instantly Ambrose was sick. The nostalgia tried to crawl out of his gut again. He started up his car's engine and drove all the way down Conduit's main road, only stopping when he hit the part where the buildings ended and the desert took over. He pulled over and parked, sucking in lungfuls of quickly cooling night air. Despite everything, he noticed how photogenic the spot was. The darkness of the desert was absolute, a depth just below the abyssal hue of the night sky, but the sun was sending one last fiery flare.

Then Ambrose spotted them: the pumpjacks. Their majesty. Metal crickets eternally dipping down to drink, silhouetted and sucking oil beneath an Instagrammable setting sun. He couldn't quite make out the name of the company painted on the sides of them. Ambrose aimed his camera at one and tried to focus.

A tumbleweed slowly filled the frame, something snagged on its brambles. He took the shot. A few more times. Zoomed in a little on the digital preview screen and grimaced: it looked like hair again. Red this time.

He thought about Malibu. About the boy's scorn for him. That kid wasn't even a member of that group anymore – the cult had dissolved not long after Ambrose's piece was published – nobody was sued. All the former members were distancing themselves from the group, largely from embarrassment. The celebrity was in rehab. The broken-nosed teenager that had burrowed into Ambrose's soul was an investment banker undergoing reconstructive facial surgery now. The cult leader was up in northern California somewhere getting into real estate.

For all their sacrifices, none of them had kept the faith.

What did Ambrose believe in? Sometimes he thought he knew. He believed in Ivy and Cal – the facts of them and their love for him – but living for them alone wasn't right. It demanded too much of them. Put them on pedestals that made them dizzy.

What did Ambrose believe in for himself? He'd always loved filthy things: dirt, rot, corruption. They were honest – the unclean truth. And there was something about forcing people to look at what was really there, about trying to make people acknowledge the decay and cruelty that society produced and yet avoided; that was a beautiful way to live.

Wasn't it?

"Hey, you looking for something?"

Ambrose turned to see who had spoken to him. A young white cis woman was standing there. The moonlight and her movement made her hands difficult to discern; they spidered, briefly multi-digited, then gloved back into normalcy. He frowned at her and tried to remember the question.

"Yeah, do you know who owns these pumpjacks?"

She shrugged. "Somebody. Who cares?"

"Do you live here?"

"Sure. I live everywhere," she said.

"What does that mean?" he asked.

She shrugged again. "Wherever I'm alive, I'm living, right?"

"I guess so," he said. "Did you know if there's a party happening in town tonight?"

"Oh," she said, "sex or drugs?"

He blinked. "Excuse me?"

"Why else would you be asking about it? You're looking for sex or drugs, right?"

"No. But I heard rumors about people using the oil out here like drugs," he said.

"Oh yeah?"

"Yeah. Is that just a rumor or is it for real?"

"So you *are* looking for drugs, then," she said.

"No," he shook his head, "answers."

"To what? You a cop?"

"No. I'm a photographer."

"Like a journalist?"

"Not anymore. Like an artist."

There was a pause, and Ambrose realized that she was staring at his camera. "Guess so," she said after a while.

HER NAME WAS Glitter and when he asked her if her parents gave it to her, she just laughed. Everything was a punchline waiting to be read. In the light he could see a stain on the front of her shirt that looked like a flower and when he pointed it out she laughed again and said yeah, it was her corsage. When he asked if she went to school, she seemed mildly insulted and said the only school around was a high school two towns over – she was twenty and studying computer science online. After that she perched on the edge of the passenger seat and gave directions while Ambrose nosed through the desert. His phone buzzed in his pocket with texts, then went still: a list of concern and well-wishes from Cal and Ivy. When he checked for bars, not even the satellites could be bothered: nothing. He was in a dead zone. He wouldn't be able to send a reply.

Someone had started a bonfire: there was always a bonfire. A fistful of cars were scattered alongside the dark road. Ambrose was directed to park beside them, so he did. When they'd parked he studied the people ringing the blaze. Young people made ragged silhouettes, formed but featureless. They danced by the flames, and only an absent sea prevented the place from being a beach. He shuddered.

"What's wrong?" Glitter asked.

That's when he realized that they'd set a pumpjack on fire.

"Oh my god – that thing could explode at any minute – they need to get away from it!"

Glitter laughed while Ambrose fumbled with his door. "No, it won't! Relax! It's totally fine – you'll see!"

Ambrose tried to believe her. He stared at the pumpjack: a dark match head in the center of the flames. He took a deep breath. He tried to remember why he was there in the first place. He picked up his camera and got out of the car.

Once his eyes adjusted to the light Ambrose realized that other things lurked in the desert: a wooden archway painted with jack-o-lanterns leering on a vine; the rusted bones of a tilt-a-whirl; a Ferris wheel asleep on its side. Ambrose took pictures of a plaster vampire slumped in his coffin. A splintered cutout of a ghost tagged to expressionlessness.

"What was this place?" he asked Glitter.

She giggled. "It *was* going to be a Halloween theme park, but then it turned into something better. Come on."

She took his elbow and tugged lightly, but he didn't hesitate; he followed her. Past the rotting games of chance and concrete tombstones with joke inscriptions carved into them. Past the groups of whispering, laughing teenagers and twentysomethings. Closer to the flaming pumpjack that loomed over them all.

As Ambrose stared, he noticed a tiny metal crown had been welded to the top of the pumpjack's long, skull-like structure. A minor detail; one that he quickly photographed. His stomach was tight. Laughter bubbled up like crude oil from the dark. Heat from the bonfire baked the side of his body that faced it, the desert a chill behind him.

Then everything stopped making sense.

The metal skull-like structure slowly and steadily turned about 45 degrees, then stopped. Like it was looking straight at Ambrose. Like it was inspecting him.

Ambrose's hands automatically took a picture. "What?" he asked, but he wasn't sure what to follow that up with. He was numb. "What is that?" he tried out. Words felt peculiar as he spoke them.

"It's a pumpjack king," Glitter giggled. "It's a mistake. It's our god now."

Ambrose looked back at the car – a shiny symbol slurring into desert sparkle at the edges of the firelight – he knew he should go. He looked back. He hesitated. Was his meaning hiding here?

At the query he received a download – the information automatically arising in his consciousness.

Everything is data: something to sample, something to replicate. Data is abundant. Data is abundance.

It's true that sometimes data becomes corrupted.

But it's not personal: nothing is personal here. Humanity is something for other people to worry about.

"Pumpjack king" – a slight slurring of intentions – not the "pumpkin king" desired outcome. A mistyped item in a search engine that turned out to be an engine of far more obscure and arcane designs. The pumpjack king was a Halloween décor item for a theme park that was never built. All wrong, but all right. A mistake that provided for the kids out in the desert who brought him fresh data.

"Our pumpjack king is lonely – you're perfect for him."

"What? No. What do you mean?"

She nodded. "The way you look at them. Your photographs. It's all over you."

Ambrose shook his head. "No," he repeated, backing away.

Glitter held her hands out like she was placating an agitated animal. "It's okay! If you don't want to do it, we'll just make slightly randomized versions of you until we find one that will. You'll be fine."

That was when he recognized another Glitter grinning out of the darkness: a twin perfect to her first in every detail, right down to the stain like a flower on her t-shirt. Glitter turned to this newcomer and kissed her deeply on the mouth, squeezing the flower tight to make the petals spread.

Ambrose looked away, nostalgia thick in him. He wanted to be home in the city. The beams of the pumpjack king were twisting, groaning, distorting in the flames. Everything was a blur or blurring, the heat from the fire echoing the warm lust pulsing in Ambrose's nervous system. He did not understand, but the sounds and the metal were summoning something submissive and libidinous from him. He did not want to be this sacrifice, but he wanted to be sacrificed. Two things roiled within him for ascendency. In horror his intentions fractured, his emotions tearing apart like layers of biological tissue, nerve-raw and bloody. He separated; he multiplied. His intestines became a cat's cradle, extended between two torsos. Above him smiling faces ringed him, mouths wide with wonder. They were so joyful.

In that moment he was their miracle. He was their meaning; and if Ambrose wanted it, he could have that meaning for himself, too.

He did not want it. He fucking hated it.

AT NIGHT the red lights fixed to the tops of distant towers winked like eyes across the long dark. Ambrose stared at the lights, his body tremoring. He tried to take a picture. Instead he vomited, his guts emptying out all over the desert floor.

EVEN THE MOONLIGHT couldn't make Conduit beautiful. It was the ugliest fucking place in the world.

THE SAME THING THAT HAPPENED TO SAM

THEY TRAIN THE WORMS TO BE AFRAID OF THE LIGHT, so it's really incredibly rare to have one come out of somebody's eye socket or something like that. The one time that I saw my mother's worm moving the pocket of dark flesh just underneath her left eye, that was a rarity. Like a solar eclipse. Most of the time the worms kept to the dark interior territory of the skull, far from any optic nerve or orifice.

Father reassured me that I wouldn't feel a thing, but what does he know? He's never had to have one put in. It's like he's cavity-free and telling me the dentist's drill won't hurt. Sam, my older brother, had one put in last year and won't talk to me anymore like he used to. When I asked him if it hurt he said no, but his voice was all wrong, just air pushed through vocal cords. I can't explain it.

Stacey Miller had her worm put in just last week. She was mostly the same afterwards. She just ignored me, the same way she has since middle school.

MOTHER AND FATHER sat me down at the kitchen table with the website on our family tablet, all swooping cursive headers on blocks of helpful text. Photographs of smiling people on anonymous lawns. Links to government websites and medical facilities.

"Mama Bear noticed that you were nervous," father said. "So we thought we'd go over the worm with you again, but as a family."

He said "as a family" but Sam wasn't there. I'd already been on this website. I'd read more than just the free pamphlets that the company had provided; I've been paying attention for years.

The nematodes were androids, their guts lined with nanites designed to digest all of the connections in my brain that my father and country had determined were "undesirable". Piece by piece, my gender and my sexuality would become food for worms before I was even buried.

I wondered again what mother was before her worm had been surgically inserted: was she non-binary like me? Or had her sexuality proved to be the problematic part of her? Maybe it was both? My father cleared his throat. I realized it must've been the third or fourth time he'd done that while I'd been sitting in front of him, and shifted my focus.

"Yes," I said, "a special nematode of my own."

"That's right, it's very special! They feed it your DNA in the lab to start your unique bond with it early. Do you know why?"

I touched the cotton ball tightly pasted to my inner elbow with a limp bandage. "So my body won't reject it," I said.

"That's right. Wow, kitten! You've sure been hitting the books!"

I looked at my mother, who intensely studied a small square of sticky paper as she tore each corner of it in half.

"What if I don't get the worm put in?"

My mother stopped tearing her sticky paper. My father put the tablet down on the table. "What did you say?" he asked me.

"What if I don't get the worm put in?" I asked. "What if I just skip the appointment?"

"Skip the appointment? After you've been publicly registered as food for worms? You're kidding, right?" he said.

"Go to the appointment," my mother said. I locked eyes with her and thought I saw a sliver of movement behind her left eye but it was impossible to tell for sure.

"You don't want to get on the wrong side of the law, do you, kitten?" he asked.

"I just wanted to know," I said.

"They'll put you in the centers, and then it gets worse," Sam said.

We all stared at him. Sam looked like he'd just come back from study group. Father looked angry, the way he had before he'd called the cops on Sam when we found out he had a boyfriend. But Sam just looked the way he always did – empty. I'd asked him once, after the worm, if he missed Nate, but he'd just been confused.

I started crying again.

"What's wrong?" mother asked.

"You're not getting agitated, are you? We can drive you to the clinic tonight – "

"No, of course not," I said, "I'm just a little nervous."

"All right," father said, "but if it gets to be too much, you can take one of the pills that the doctor gave you. Let me know and I'll get one from the cabinet."

$$\mathcal{P}_x^{\circ}$$

IT WAS ALMOST LIKE A PARTY. That night I ate food that I hardly tasted, swallowing dutifully. I kept repeating the thoughts that I loved most in chaotic cacophony, but chaos was interrupted by the most mundane things: opening a present from father and mother (a dress I would never usually wear, pre-worm), a toast, a group photo in front of a cake. The cake had a pink icing worm wriggling in and out of bold letters that spelled "Baby's First Worm".

I threw up in the bathroom.

$\partial_x \%$

THE CLINIC WAS A BEIGE BLANKNESS. I am thankful for that.

$\partial_x \%$

SO MUCH IN my brain now is beautiful worm shit.

It's the kind of beautiful I always hated: all empty surfaces. Glass bubbles breaking open inside me to cut everything tender apart.

$\partial_x \%$

AT NIGHT the worm chews on my memories, reordering them into more acceptable patterns. I was never attracted to Stacey Miller I never kissed her behind the snack stand at the softball field I was always watching home runs. Boys running in a square that they call a diamond. The lawn was so green and well-groomed it looked artificial.

In order to outrun the worm, I must think new thoughts: stronger, stranger, queerer thoughts than ever before. I think gay things all the time, filling my moments with so many of them that the worm rasps noisily along the inside of my skull with all the eating it has to do.

I make my worm busy with the business of myself, planning my infinite revenges.

EXPENSIVE MEAT

I don't want abs
I just want someone to love my softness
with the skin of their tongue
the heat of their teeth
slow, + tender cooking
me like expensive meat

IN RESPONSE TO YOUR EMAIL

We drove around Coronado all afternoon, our relationship a dead body stinking up the back seat. I didn't smoke weed yet or I would've been smoking; little hits from a glass pipe to make the thong riding up my ass more fun. But I didn't smoke weed yet. I was still young and tender from mother's unwanted valiums and percocets. Wincingly drug-shy. It would take college and a ring of men I wanted to bond with, that moment of warm dumbfuck solidarity to reawaken my curiosity and coax my closeted trans masc ass to puff puff pass and feel absolutely nothing. I was assured that weed rarely got you high the first time, that the THC needed time to build up in your system – so at least I had something to look forward to.

But this was eons before that first toke, my biochemical Cenozoic era, and it was crowded in Coronado; the little beaches occupied, the legal parking options already taken. It was hot. Desert hot even by the sea. Like the water meant nothing to the sun. Maybe it didn't. They said there really was a sea in the desert, the Salton Sea; artificially bloated and full of dead gulls that had eaten the polluted and salt-sick fish. I wanted to take a trip there, but he wasn't so sure about going. I thought about waves of salt and bones rolling and rolling, breaking down into a fine, calcium-rich sand. White powdered beaches like lines of bone cocaine. Someone was grilling a hot dog. I couldn't see the sand from here, just cars in the parking lots. I started telling him we should do something else or he started telling me we should do something else: we were both done with San Diego even though we couldn't leave yet. If we left now we'd get stuck in traffic, and then he'd get anxious and start jerking off in the driver's seat. He never wanted my help when that happened, he'd just masturbate: his eyes sticky and glued to the road, indifferent to whether I watched or not. Whether anyone noticed him or didn't. I think a part of him wanted to get caught, to have his shame catch up to him and strike him down like an angry god in a cheap cop costume. I think I wanted to go to the porn superstore again. I was working my way through the kinks. I'd already read the classics. I was twenty, and my primary hobby was looking for myself in really strange places.

He said "fine", but when it got cold and I rolled the window up all I could smell was rotten corpse meat.

WE DIDN'T END up at the porn superstore. We went back to his house. His parents were out doing something normal like getting groceries or eating dinner. We had hours to kill. To throttle with our stubby, dirty fingers. We got back into his car. Or no. That was later. Or earlier.

Can't you keep your story straight? No, dude, I'm fucking queer.

Something happened, and I ended it. That's what I know. You don't need the details. I walked away, but not far enough or fast enough, and it happened again (*did I let it happen again?*), so I ended it again, but harder this time; slamming the door in between our connection to burn not just bridges but whole towns cities *countries* down in my haste to run away. My guilt and shame hissing: "stupid, stupid – how could you trust him a second time?" (*how could I let it happen again?*) forgetting that even con men get conned. Even hustlers get hustled. And sometimes you want to believe that someone you love is capable of changing for the better (ha), when all they can do is let you know how hurt they are by hurting you (ah).

Sometimes you lie to yourself without even realizing it. I know I have. Haven't you?

So SOMETHING HAPPENED, and my face fell off.

I'm not blaming it all on him: I'd spent years wearing down on the thing – tugging at the edges trying to rip it off, or applying so many elaborate and painful masks (some made entirely of broken glass or bent nails, things that were purely torturous to wear, private masochisms that were meant to absolve or enlighten me, I forget which nowadays) – that I am fully conscious of my contribution to the way things went down. I know what I did. I know where I went wrong. Still: that doesn't mean that I deserved to lose my face. I was twenty for fuck's sake.

I couldn't find it, not for years. No matter where I searched, or how hard I tried. When I told my mother that I'd lost it she said that in a past life we had been lovers, and now she could become the face that I had lost. She was so eager to fill me in on the details of our reincarnations, no matter how much I begged her to stop. So I stopped answering the phone when she called. When I told my father what she'd said he assured me that she was a liar, and he was the only one in this world who would ever love me, I'd see it was so in the end. So.

I learned how to see without my eyes – but only a little bit. I couldn't see much, just a meaty smudge, some lights dancing in vague patterns. It was too painful to focus for very long on any particular thing. I turned up the brightness on every device I owned with a screen and switched to audiobooks. I'd draw my eyes on with makeup in the morning, careful to pencil in the irises and apply thick white dots to symbolize light, and the makeup would be gone by noon and so would my eyes. At least I could wear a face mask to hide the absence of my nose and mouth. My pores were breathing for me now; miniscule gusty inhalations puffing vigorously on the surface of my skin. As for eating, I discovered that I could slowly absorb the nutrients of anything that I touched for a prolonged period of time if I focused on the object. I'd hold a french fry and watch it dwindle down to nothing like a melting stick of butter in my palm. But I couldn't taste what I was absorbing, so it wasn't nearly as fun as eating used to be. I absorbed a lot more vegetables than I would've normally consumed, and that was good for my cholesterol, which admittedly had been a little high the last time I checked the number with a doctor. I thought about going to see my doctor and asking for her opinion on facial reconstruction surgeries, but my health insurance was shit and I didn't have that kind of pay-to-play money. What was I going to do – ask my parents for help? They were two faces on a worn, faceless coin. One so unidentifiable no one would honor it as currency.

Eventually I stopped looking for my old face. What was the point? Life kept happening even if I didn't have one. I kept waking up, absorbing things, listening to music, attending classes, working at the community college's radio station helping the grizzled dude in the booth fix the website. Something was always breaking on the website. In my spare time I made gifs, miniature animations of spinning records and melting stars. Soda cans full of lube, effervescent with condom balloons. Roses that wept sparrows. I crowded my brain with everything that screamed. I scraped my vocal cords thin with screaming. Pain was my alchemy, and I hurt until my throat became a crucible, capable of transmuting blood clots to boluses. I swallowed every lump. I swallowed everything back then.

If I was honest, the eyes I drew on every day looked like shit. If I was honest, I didn't think I deserved anything better at the time.

And that's when I met you, bruised and defeated, a little drunk like me, and I was wanting something like a color I'd never seen before to enter my life. (Do you know how funny that is? I thought I'd never seen you before.) We met at a party and you asked me what I did for a living and I said I was decorative and you laughed like I hoped you would. But when you asked me my name I just changed the subject. It wasn't a topic I was particularly interested in. But you were. And your interest in me was fascinating because I hadn't been interested in that asshole/myself for ages (but you were).

Appalled at your bad taste, I smeared my eyes with a fist and pulled down my face mask to show you the smooth featurelessness of myself.

"I'm a freak," I said, but the words were muffled, and when you can't cry, every tear you can't shed is a tiny knife tearing you quietly apart. Every little mermaid knows that.

You laughed and pulled me into your arms and told me that some people shed faces like deer shed antlers: in time my face would grow back again. Didn't I know? I did not know. You kissed me where my lips used to be. Stunned, I pushed back against you, the only part of a kiss I could still give.

You ASKED me to tell you what I'd always dreamed of doing but had never done, and in your arms all I could think of was bone cocaine.

So you drove me to the Salton Sea and I made you take

pictures of us to look at later, maybe, when I had my eyes back. I oriented myself at the water and tried to feel something, but without my nose I could not smell the rot; without my mouth I could not taste the salt. Standing in front of that beach felt, more or less, like standing in front of a television set with a picture of a beach playing on it. I could have stayed at home. I could have spent nothing, gone nowhere, and felt exactly like this. It was so wasteful, being me.

That was when we fought for the first time.

I'm sorry. I fought you because I didn't want my old face, and that wasn't your fault. You were the messenger, and I didn't want to hear it. I only knew that I wanted a new face, one of my own design, and if the old one was going to grow back, and had been growing back all the while, who knows how much time I had left to make a face of my own? I searched online, but the answers were all over the place: I could have days, weeks, years left before a new one grew in. I made you drop me off at a friend's house. Later you sent me an email but I didn't open it.

You couldn't rescue me, do you understand? You weren't qualified for the job. I had to descend: so far I'd been Hades, coveting the Persephone of myself. Now I had to become Demeter. Ugh.

A parent at my age? I trembled at the thought; I was too young to be a parent, too irresponsible. I got drunk to prove it, but that didn't prove anything. The next morning when I woke up, hangover-thick, I realized I was going to be late to my history class so I skipped it. Decided to stay home instead. The radio station's website would be a little more broken than usual today – so mote it be. This was the day for breaking things.

ALONE IN MY apartment I broke myself anew.

I rubbed my palms along the flat plane where my face should be. I'd put a pair of scissors, a kitchen knife, and a bottle of what I hoped was antiseptic within arm's reach. But before I used any tools, I wanted to start out with the basics.

I fingered the surface where my face used to be: flesh, pimpled and downy. The cartilage of my nose was gone, but the bridge remained, a bony knob. If I applied pressure, I felt the blades of my cheekbones, the cobblestones of my covered teeth.

If I had been logical, I would have attempted to recreate my eyes first, but in that moment I let emotions guide my surgical hand: I proceeded with my mouth first. I tapped the skin that covered my teeth, then started rubbing my index finger horizontally at the invisible line where my top and bottom rows met. I brought my finger inwards, like a shallow gag, until I felt the thick, tender meat of my skin against the tips of my incisors.

Before I could think too much about it I bit as hard as I could. One bite. My mouth was crowded with a scream and blood and the lump of myself but I kept chewing, biting, aggressively tearing a hole until my tongue touched air again, until my teeth were bared, until there was a raw seam wide enough to purge the hot lump and blood and sickness through. Vomit stung my new aperture.

The pain was everything, terrible: if I didn't continue now I'd never continue.

Now I grabbed the knife. Blood trembled over lips like butchery. I brought the blade to the outer edge of my left eye socket, and pressed the tip in, just a slight, shallow cut, then sliced. Blood and clear fluid pinkly erupted from the wound. My vision was a murky window of ocular fluid, blinking against the brightness. I quickly repeated my surgery: blade to the edge of my right socket, the shallow cut, the slicing. The pain was my face and my face was the pain. My face was all pain. Everything was pink water and bile. I dropped the knife and lost consciousness.

WHEN I WOKE up the light was different. Hours had passed. I had to fight the new scabs that had crept over my eyelids and mouth while I slept. I rubbed and picked at the painful grit that had formed there, ripping bits of dried blood cells away until I could take a look at a mirror and see how far I'd come.

The work was rough, and instead of eye whites something the color of skinned grapes rested in my eyesockets, the bright red dot of a raw optic nerve nestled in the heart of each scoop.

I still didn't have a nose. There was so much work left to be done! In weary frustration I gripped the flesh in the center of my freshly-cut features and began yanking outward. It hurt, and as soon as I released the meat, it fell back against the bones flatly. Gritting my molars together, I continued yanking and pulling, working my lump of flesh for hours, intentionally mangling the meat until everything was horribly sore and tender and a purple and reddish bruise had swollen up to form a modest peak in the center of my face in progress.

I picked up the scissors, parted the blades an inch, and punctured the bottom of the lumpy bruise. Blood gouted out, the ferrous brine of it burned my sinuses. Blood clattered down to paint my new scabby lips. I bled, and my bleeding became breathing; bubbles of snot, pink clots of mucus purged from me. I sagged, ragged and salty, hitching on hiccups. Like the pricks of fresh rain on dead ground, I wept.

It had been so long I had forgotten how good it felt to cry.

FINALLY, I saw you with my own eyes.

I studied the picture of us, taken together as we stood on a landlocked shore. You were faceless, like I had been only hours ago. Your eyes were well-drawn illustrations. Two trompe l'oeil tattoos, taut on a blank stretch of weathered skin. Your jaw stretched with a similarly tattooed smile. I grinned back at you. I understood you better now. I finally knew what you were afraid of.

I couldn't stop grinning.

My joy was blood weeping into my naked eyes; alive like licking caviar from a Salton Sea fish; alive like blistering sores exploding, corrupting, blooming on my tongue at your tongue's touch (a man can dream).

So I answered your email.

MY BODY BECAME A LABYRINTH

Menstruation is an infinite crime because it means that life goes on – the awful, shocking pain of it, and blood reminds us of this debasing truth: we were embodied.

So when the doctor mentioned scheduling the date of my abortion and I immediately thought: *Out, damned spot! Out I say!* my subconscious had already incriminated me. *Murderer*, my mind insinuated and, more condemning yet: *Lady*.

My body became a labyrinth, starting at my nipples, which were suddenly ridged by squiggly hedges of flesh that I thought at first puckered up from the chill of my apartment but the ridges kept growing, asserting patterns, dropping flesh, spreading outward to make two circular mazes of my breasts within minutes. I lifted a hand to touch the right one but the act of lifting my arm unraveled its meaning into long switch-back corridors of red raw muscle and bone tiling: more mazes. My legs went weak, as if they were similarly growing undone, and as I fell backwards the smallest part of me slid back, too, from a space right between my eyes, harrowing my vision smaller and smaller as I went, ass-first, out of the back of my brain and down the lumpy, bumpy knobs of my spinal cord. Down, down the dark slide of bone I fell until I hit the imposing cathedral of my ribcage. I was a wet splot, gray and red, my limbs short and new and gummy. A long ropey tail of bone sprouted from the back of me and connected me to my spinal cord, which was reasserting itself into the kind of unscalable steps you might find at an art gallery to make a point about accessibility in design.

Everything to the horizon of myself had become a labyrinth; I could only imagine the state of my intestinal tract.

Distantly, I heard a faint feral cry, new and needful. I shivered in fear. Somehow I knew that the being that screamed was as hopelessly lost as I was.

SHALL I commit thee to traumatic memory? Shall I bind thee, Spot, to this page and make thee unscourgeable at last?

I THOUGHT I WAS DYING. I woke up in the middle of the night covered in sweat, panic gripping me, and ran to the bathroom.

I vomited blood. Salty, warm, inexplicable. I'd eaten a benign pasta for dinner that wasn't even discernable in this cartoonish volley of gore. In fear I watched the toilet go red red red. This was it, my dying time.

Vomiting blood wasn't a sign of COVID, though, so we contacted a doctor over the phone for advice.

W$_E$ $_{CALL}$ $_{IT}$ "$_{THE}$ S$_{COTTISH}$ $_{PLAY}$" instead of *Macbeth* when we don't want the eyes of the angels on us.

Lady Macbeth can be considered an allegory for menstruation; the blood on her hands menstrual, her only crime her sinister nature, allotted to her from apple to Eve to lip to hip. She was never supposed to be good. She never could have been.

T$_{HE}$ $_{TELEDOCTOR}$ $_{ASKED}$ me when I'd last menstruated, decided I wasn't pregnant, then prescribed a couple of different medications. Sometimes people just vomited blood, apparently. I picked up the medications from the pharmacy. The bottles were covered with warning stickers in big, bold print: DO NOT TAKE WHILE PREGNANT. But I wasn't pregnant, I was vomiting blood at night. And during the day, now, too. But never in the morning. And morning sickness just happens in the morning, right? That's why they call it 'morning sickness'?

I took my pills and they took away the blood. For a while.

I $_{REMAINED}$ in the shelter of my ribcage for a long time. I studied the sunset-colored light that blazed like a McGuffin from the general direction of my cunt. I could not remember what a home looked like – either my own or the general concept. In the end I decided that home was irrelevant. There was no need to return to one, or really to proceed anywhere.

My long tail seemed to function somewhat like an umbilical cord, and I felt no physical urges or needs. No hunger. No fatigue. Seedlike I hoped that the earth would quake and tumble soil down upon my form. I wanted burial. Decomposition. I waited and watched the light.

I FELT A CONCENTRATION OF HEAT, a throbbing solidity inside of me, and feared cancer. I pressed my gut against the mattress and thought about chemotherapy and surgery and how inadequate my health insurance coverage currently was.

And then I let the fact of that inadequacy sink in and took a fucking pregnancy test.

WHY COULDN'T the earth rise up to swallow me whole? Earthquakes happen in California all the time. But the light is steady overhead. The ground beneath me firm. Maybe I'm not in California.

MY PARTNER/INSEMINATOR offered his hand in the car and I think I took it, I really do. I tried to leave my limited perspective behind and live in his for a while. He was sad. His sadness was something I could swim in – a strong current I already felt. It rushed and roared and thrummed downhill. Madcap we went through it but my sorrow kept getting stuck on an eddy, a diversion of still water sticky with mosquito larvae. Something rotten just for me.

Banquo said to Macbeth, like an asshole: "...You should be women, /And yet your beards forbid me to interpret /That you are so." If my own face was beard-thick, I think unkindly to myself, strangers would be forbidden to interpret me as woman.

Overhead my ribs loom, monolithic. The golden light is burnt mauve at the edges. An ache-like emptiness opens inside of me and I instinctively glance back at my tail. Just as I fear, it is beginning to rot. Fresh patches of green and purple decay blister open. Frantically I dash forward, trying to outrun the mulching of my own flesh, but the tail goes taut with tension until – pop! – I reach the limit of its length and it disconnects from me. At the base of my spine yellowish skin, rough and thick, has collected where the tail used to be. I try to scrape the skin off but my new hands are all gummy, finger-nail-free stubs. The flesh squishes beneath my soft pads like feta.

I am mouthless, but hungry. The crying is still out there, frail and piercing.

I start to walk the labyrinth.

I named you "Spot" in secret. It's a horrible name – the name for a dog. The kind of wretched nickname I would come up with for a close friend after we'd been out all night drinking and spilled hot sauce on ourselves. You're the "red eye" in a "red eye flight". You're the dot in a 7-Up can. An empty ubiquity. A casual haunting of myself.

I BEGIN my journey down through my right breast, my hand trailing along the walls as I go. I think as I proceed through it that the person in charge has really let things get out of hand; the corridors are endless. It's honestly too much to deal with. This used to be so much more manageable.

In the soft space between my breasts I find myself in deeper melancholy: I would give anything to see the skin here planted with hair like a field of long-dead weeds. But there is only more labyrinthine breast ahead. The mauve-gold McGuffin light. The piteous screaming.

I proceed ahead.

LADY MACBETH WILL NEVER STOP WASHING her hands until she is debased and her protective skin gives way and she reaches raw meat. The rawness is the point – it becomes her sacrifice – something to offer up to heaven to infect or cure as heaven deems fit.

That's because it's always nicer to have someone else to judge us, to decide if we're really worth keeping around or not.

I HUNGER but there is nothing to eat and I don't have a mouth, anyway. I'm a gray, small thing, still lost in my body. I can't tell exactly which organ I am currently inside of, but think that it might be a kidney. I wish there was starlight. Starlight would be preferable to all this rusty gold. I keep walking because I feel no particular urge to rest. The emptiness is there, driving me on and forward. A hollow ache.

I AM NOT A LADY. I never have been, and never could be.

I had forgotten the importance of my gender, somehow. For years I had distanced myself from my body and the significance of it, only going to health clinics for STD checks and emergencies. My body was a distraction, or a discomfort, or an embarrassing abundance. I was depressed, and resigned to living in a form that I wanted to constantly ignore. It was like somehow I was puppeteering my own corpse around, *Weekend at Bernie's*-style, and nobody had caught on yet. I believed that gender was for other people. Good for the youths. Great for folks who wanted to participate in life. But I just wanted to grieve and surround myself with a few nice accomplishments before I died – a kind of death before dying – and vomiting blood felt appropriate and right. A good way to go out. Dramatic and messy and poetic (after all as a horror writer my voice is a variety of vomited blood).

But instead of dying I was having an abortion and living, living, living. The earth was not quaking to bury me; I was the earthquake. I horrified myself.

THE LADY STAGE whispers at me: "That which cries 'Thus thou must do,' if thou have it, /And that which rather thou dost fear to do, /Than wishest should be undone."

Fucking bitch.

I FOLLOW THE SCREAM. I follow it and follow it until I don't remember why I'm following it anymore. There's only the screaming and my hunger. My appetite and the appetizing. I am afraid of myself, afraid that I am going to eat the pitiful, delicious thing at the end of the labyrinth's maze. I'm afraid that I am all selfishness, all appetite, with nothing loving left. There is no tenderness remaining in me, I think, and the punishing puzzle does not contradict me. It cannot. I do fear my own nature – thinking it too empty of the milk of human kindness despite whatever my breasts might be doing.

I must go faster. I try to. The crying is increasing in volume, and my womb is not inviting, it is an endless maze doubling back on itself, as tangled and confused as I am. I am lost, I have been lost since the beginning, but now the reality of being lost sinks into me and I feel as lost as I truly am. The cry is loud. Louder. Increasing in volume to vibrate the walls of the labyrinth itself.

I turn left and the sound is gone. The narrow corridors of the labyrinth have been replaced with a vast, paved space, circular in shape. Other routes seem to branch off from this space, subtly.

I am shocked at how empty it is. There's a solitude to this place, a loneliness so profoundly peaceful that I instantly understand the appeal of it. The McGuffin light is sunny overhead.

I don't realize that I have acquired a mouth, that my flesh has split to form two gummy lips, until I am smiling.

Euphoric I ate fast food and truly tasted it. The salt on my fries stung my tongue with not just salt but shock. Soda's syrup was a kind of nectar, far too sweet for my mortal mouth. I drank it down fast before the ice melted, leaving it for my stomach to contend with.

I touched my flesh and found the sensation pleasurable. The form of my body was flawed, but infinitely mutable, and mine. Powerful. A potential engine.

I wept because Spot was not there to rejoice with me. They were out, damned Spot.

Alone, I knew what I wanted.

The walls of the labyrinth bent forward, listening to me as I rebuilt myself. My consciousness slid backwards through the maze, up and through and out again, then up the rattle of my spinal column, into the roof of my own skull once more. Muscles knit around bones. Fat fondled muscle. In the end my body couldn't comply with all of my requests, but promised to listen attentively. To drink their hormones. The important thing is that I would start paying attention to them again. No more silence. I am here for them.

There is a moment of male-to-male impregnation in *Macbeth* (angels look upon me now). It's brief, and you might very well miss it in a casual read. There is an exchange between Duncan and Banquo, a dialogue fertile with their masculine friendship. Duncan says "I have begun to plant thee and will labor /To make thee full of growing".

I plant this in myself.

ALIVE, alive, alive again! I am reborn unto myself; in forgiveness and love I hold my body and live.

I am non-binary. I am trans masc. I grip each moment I live in a fist. I refuse to let go again, even if the pain of it leaves my palms weeping blood. I attend to my gender with the loving tenderness of a parent, and I think that, given the right circumstances, even I could be pregnant again one day.

TWO PRESSED FLOWERS IN A BOOK
OF FILTH

It was going to happen someday and now someday is here, and the garbage is coming down on us, falling like a prophecy, grating eyelids away with aluminum can precision, pressing us flat like fists pressing shit together. You are nearby, but undetectable. You are gone; already lost to me.

I can't tell you I love you. I can't tell you goodbye. You were there, and now you aren't. There's only trash left behind: everything garbage. Gently crushing us. Killing us.

It's been so long since anyone we know has been down to our branch. Since any friends came by to share a story or some mushrooms. No one will find our bodies in time to rescue us. There's no *deus ex machina* in our near futures. No benevolent god steering an Excavator or a Crane. Our rusty saints have long abandoned us to our stinking piles. Their sigils and songs forgotten.

I'm suffocating and searching for your scent in the pile. Just a scrap of you, no matter how foul. The fall tore our locked fists asunder, and I keep driving my fingers into the ground glass and maggots nearby, but the reassuring wriggle of your hand eludes me, and I am dying alone. With you, but alone. Near you, but alone.

At the Hub you kept smiling at me and I was the luckiest man in the entire pile that night. I still think that I'm lucky. We never went to all those places you wanted to go see. We never went upside – I'm sorry. People always say that the sun is such a pretty shade of red. Like a wound bleeding from impossibly high up above. You would have loved that. I would have loved you loving that. I love you.

I'm screaming but the plastic skins of past purchases stopper up the sound. I'm choking on pure capitalism, and so are you. Maybe you're screaming, too. It's uncomfortable. It's a comfort. I wish I could imagine your salvation, but I don't want to die lying to myself, so here are some truths instead: we were gay and we loved each other the best we could, and that love meant something, even when the world buried us underneath its filth. All the garbage in the world can't ruin what we had. What we have, right now. For now.

Somewhere far above us the billionaires are burning up on their way to outer space. I bet their exploding rockets look like LED lights after an earthquake. Like something to celebrate when everything falls apart. I wish I could show you. I wish we could go see.

THE THING THAT MOVES THE MEAT

THEY LIKE ME, BUT THEY DO NOT LOVE ME. THEY CAN'T love me; they are in love with the invisible thing that moves my meat.

They explained it to me when I met them. "I'm painting the spiritual limbic. The arcane liquidity that we only bear witness to in actions."

"What?" I asked them. They wore a single playing card torn in half as earrings – the jack of clubs split down the middle. Their sidecut's fade was so clean I wanted to run my index finger down its incline into the soft divot behind their ear.

"The invisible thing that moves your meat," they said.

"My soul?"

They shrugged. "Whatever you'd like to call it."

"You're trying to paint souls?"

They frowned. "I'm trying to decipher the anatomy of the unseen."

"Okay," I said. "What does my soul look like?"

"Never mind," they said. "This isn't going to work."

"What? Wait, what did I say?"

"You're too impatient."

"I'm not," I said. "I'm sorry if I said something that bothered you, but I promise that I can be very patient. I've sat for a lot of artists."

They looked at me, their eyes serious and steady, then said. "Get up and move around."

I stood up from the stool in the empty college classroom. It was late, that indigo hour where the lights on the campus buzzed on in orange and the crowds had thinned to clusters of night classes that you could hear, muffled and remote through the walls.

"How should I move?" I asked them.

"How should I know? Just move."

I decided to treat it like modeling for gesture sketches, and started snapping into different poses, only a little faster than usual. I arched my back. I knelt down. I bowed. I pointed at a window. I clasped both of my hands around my neck.

"Yes," they said, "that's it! That's fine. Oh god, yes – beautiful!"

And I tried not to let their words matter but each one landed in me like a spark; I was soon warm with the heat of their casually delivered compliments. Something I had not felt in years. They were looking at me. Really looking. Really seeing me.

I tried to remind myself that this feeling wasn't real, just a skittering thing across the brain. A release of chemicals into my bloodstream; an accelerated heartrate; a sudden stutter in my respiratory function.

And then they weren't looking anymore. I felt the absence of their gaze upon my flesh before I saw it; an abrupt chill puckering my exposed skin.

"That will do," they said. "The position's yours if you want it, but I can't pay you much."

I laughed. "You're an artist. Of course you can't pay me much."

Their face reddened, the tendons on the back of their

hands went stark; I'd found a raw nerve. "I'll be able to pay you more once my vision gets more traction – "

"I just wanted to work with you," I said.

"Really?" they said. And I felt it again, first as heat then seen: their looking.

"Yes," I said. They kept looking. Their warmth burned me.

But then they stopped looking. It was late. The interview was over. I had to go home. I hurried and got on the train, sliding over the streets of Santa Monica like a cartoon snake, the X-rayed mouse of myself looking out a window. Lost even though I knew the way home.

$$\mathcal{P}_x^{\%}$$

My studio apartment is off the books because it's actually a one-car garage that the obscenely wealthy building owner converted into a studio after viewing too many tiny home shows. The bathroom is the afterthought of an afterthought. The night the artist hired me I stared at the sink as I brushed my teeth. I kept the bathroom mirror in my peripheral vision; I model for artists but I don't like looking at myself. A lot of my exes think that's funny, but I don't. I spat toothpaste at the rusty drain, rinsed the glob away with equally rusty water.

It was needing to be looked at that was the problem – that desire, gnawing and demeaning. The modeling work usually fed that. I was accustomed to being observed, really; didn't people look at me every day?

But they didn't. That was the thing. Even when you stood in front of someone naked to the skin and shaking from the cold they could look and only see the vaguest hint of what was really there. A faint outline distorted with their own style and intention. Most people only saw what they were looking for: it was almost impossible for them to witness what was really in front of them at any given time, unless –

I washed my mouth out with water from the tap. Spat it out. A chill from the poured concrete of the floor knived up my legs.

Only the curious really saw things. Or those who cared enough to look. I wanted the latter to be true; I wanted them to care so badly. That was the other thing. Was my desire lying to me? Telling me something I only wanted to think? My thumb twitched over glass. On the surface of my phone they were there: everything about them. The white Latinx non-binary 30-something artist taking the art world by the throat. Their blue eyes and disheveled sidecut and freckle-dotted skin. The critical acclaim of their Out of Tune touring show of several spirit radios that they placed in different rooms of supposedly haunted houses around Los Angeles. The success of their Living Tarot show before that – with hired actors representing the cards of the tarot deck randomly appearing to individual spectators in peepshow rooms at the insertion of a dollar in a slot.

I know too much about them. I already knew too much about them before I showed up for the interview. But my knowledge does nothing to comfort me. It's just an assortment of facts that brings me no closer to them than this job will.

THEY'VE DECIDED to draw me at their studio, a small empty room that the college lets them use. I was unclear about the details of the arrangement that they have with the school, and didn't press them about it. I arrived early, hoping to talk to them. Too early – they weren't there yet. I took out my phone and unintentionally accessed my camera. The camera was reversed, showing me a picture of my own face, horrified and stabbing at the screen to turn the damn thing off.

In the middle of all that, they showed up.

They stared, and I flushed with embarrassment but not the heat of their gaze and that's when I realized that they were staring in my direction, but they weren't staring at me. Their brow furrowed as I stabbed the phone. Their fingers kept reaching for their pencil case then hesitating. I put the phone away, and their hand relaxed.

"Hello," I said.

"Yes," they said, nodding at me. "Are you ready?" They withdrew a key from their pocket to open the door. The classroom had desks pushed up against a far wall and little else inside of it.

"Of course," I said, even though I wasn't.

DISROBING WAS UNEVENTFUL – they rummaged around in their pencil case and arranged sketchbooks while I stripped to my underwear. When they appeared to be done I walked to the center of the room and started moving randomly like I had before.

And then they drew me.

But no, that's not accurate. They didn't draw me at all. They weren't even looking at me; I couldn't feel any warmth from their gaze touching me. When I was able to peek at them I confirmed it – they were looking right though me. Peering intently at something just above or beyond me. Fascinated with my spiritual limbic.

"What are you doing? Keep moving," they said.

I kept moving. I knelt. I covered my eyes. I touched my toes. It became a kind of dance, odd and rhythmless. Their hand constantly moved across the pages of their sketchbooks. There was an instinctual quality to their gesture, reminiscent of automatic writing or the motions of sleepwalkers. Their own dance, different but in disjointed time with my own. There was an intimacy to this matched biology, a primal duality, but then I remembered the invisible subject in the room, the one that they were actually drawing, and I could only feel cold. I was shivering, my shivers moving their pencil across the page until they stopped and tore the page free, crumpled it in their fist.

"Are you cold? You're not moving much. Take a break," they said.

And that flicker of care, quick across me, made me jump with its heat. I stood in front of them, absolutely confused, as they stretched and took a sip of water from a bottle they'd brought with them. I put my robe on, and headed towards their sketches, intent on taking a look for myself.

"Oh no, not yet. This is going to take a while. I'll show you the finished pieces, I promise. But not these," they said.

"Oh, okay," I said. But it wasn't. Not a bit.

THAT NIGHT I went home to yet another message on my phone from my mother misgendering me. The only person I had come out to, and she never bothered to get it right. It was difficult to imagine anyone bothering to get it right. Anyone really seeing me completely. There were moments of recognition, slim like waning moons, but they seemed too few and far between. Most days were overcast with bullshit like this one.

I deleted the phone message and tried to look at profiles on the dating app I'd downloaded. People were interested in me, or more accurately interested in the pictures that I'd chosen to post, because I barely had the courage to put anything actually about myself up there. My 33 years of age were there. My interest in art museums. I used to have my career posted, but too many bizarro inquiries get sent to an "artist's model". I tried to focus on the multitudes of faces on my phone screen, but they're the one I wanted to look at and eventually I gave up and put the phone away.

"Keep moving," they said.

"I'm tired," I said. I wasn't tired, but I still said it.

Frustrated, they put their charcoal stick aside. "Fine, take a break," they said.

"Why don't you draw me instead? Just for fun. It'll make it easier on me."

They frowned. "Take your break," they said. They got up and collected their sketches together. Took a sip from their ever-ready water bottle.

I put my robe on. Went up to them. "Any finished sketches today?"

"Not yet."

"That's a shame. I'd really like to see them."

They scrubbed the shaved part of their head with their stained fingers, smearing charcoal into their stubble. "It's not happening any time soon," they said.

"Well, can you at least tell me what my soul looks like?"

More charcoal darkened their stubble. "Like energy. Like raw forceful *power*."

That shocked me. "Really?"

"I don't lie about the spiritual limbic."

"Does it look like electricity?"

"No."

"What does it look like?" I asked. But they just sat down and frowned at me. Took out a ballpoint pen and started chewing on the end of it.

"It looks like something inside of myself," they said finally, when the pause had gone so long I'd half-forgotten what I asked.

"What do you mean?" I said, but they wouldn't answer me.

THEY CAN'T LOVE ME. It's impossible for them to love me. How can they love this jumbled assortment of sacrospinal liga- ment, acromion, and gastrocnemius? This absolute chaos of blood vessels and bacteria? This disgusting pile of living, dying, breathing meat?

They love invisible things. Divinity only they can see. I've asked to look at their sketches but they refuse to show me anything, time and time again. They insist on my patience. They aren't ready yet. At this point I don't know if they'll ever be ready. If their big gallery show is even going to happen. It's been months since they first started drawing me.

I don't care if the show happens, but I want to know what I look like to them more than anything else. I hate that I want to know. I hate how much I want it.

I DID an adult photo set but my energy was lackluster and the photographer that I usually work with saw it and called it off early. She told me to go home and gave me fifty bucks more than we agreed on. When I objected she folded my hand around the money and said I needed the rest. Made me agree that I wouldn't call her until I worked on myself. I wanted to cry right there in her studio, but I didn't.

I wish I could feel that powerful energy that they saw moving me. I wish that I could see it. Some days I want to see it even more than I want to know how they see me. As if knowing the shape of my soul would clarify all the murk I slog through, or at least be the kind of secret that made slogging through the murk worthwhile.

It feels like everything I want right now is in their sketchbook. Everything.

FOR OUR FINAL modeling session they wanted to draw me in a different room on the college campus than the one we usually used. They gave me directions but I got lost twice, and when I arrived at the numbered auditorium, they kept giving me angry looks that made me blush.

"I got lost," I explained.

"I don't have this room for very long," they said. "Just an hour."

When I entered I realized that it wasn't just an auditorium; there was a raised wooden stage bordered with red curtains at the bottom of the tiered plush seating. This was one of the theater department's stages.

"Go on the stage," they said.

I shivered. Descended the narrow path of stairs between the seats to the bottom. A spotlight went on, highlighting the gold of the polished wooden boards. I looked back but couldn't see them behind the flare of the spotlight. I disrobed in the shadows just offstage, hesitated, then removed my underwear. They hadn't requested it this time, but I wanted to be as exposed to them as I possibly could be.

I mounted the stage. The wood creaked beneath me. I looked up and saw only the spotlight. I shielded my eyes, squinting at the seats.

"I'm here," they said. I couldn't see them, but they sounded close by. "Start whenever you're ready."

I nodded, and began my disjointed dance. I swept my leg wide. Clenched my limbs inward like a fist. Hefted an unseen lance. Soon I could hear them join me; invisible graphite scratching across invisible paper. A duet of obstruction, connected at my hips. I thrust my hips as if I could tug them closer to me. Looked up. And saw.

A form so innately mutable it was almost indescribable, but powerful and raw, pulsing –

I fell down. The back of my head struck the solid wood of the stage. All of my perception shut off, abruptly replaced with darkness. When my head rebounded and hit the wood a second time, my vision returned. They knelt over me, eclipsing the spotlight and the hideous, perfect glowing thing behind them with the limbs of a star.

"Are you all right?" they asked me. "Are you hurt? Talk to me."

"I see it," I said. It loomed over us both. When it briefly enmeshed with the restless form of their own soul I felt a dart of heat; they were looking at me.

"You see your arcane liquidity?" they asked. "Do you see mine?"

"Yes," I said.

"You do? Tell me! What does it look like?"

I blinked. "You can't see it?"

"No!" I shivered and they peeled their jacket off and handed it to me. "I've done everything I can to widen my spiritual apertures! I've meditated. Taken mind-altering substances. Consulted countless advisors. But I can only see the spiritual limbic of a few."

"Really?" I asked. They reached out to touch the curve of my cheek and I witnessed the fleshy, wet fabric of their soul guide their hand there. It pulsed arrhythmically. Expanded and contracted at whim.

"Yes," they said, reaching up to touch the ropey meat of my own glistening soul. As their fingers connected with my ethereal tissue I cried out with pleasure. "I've only fallen in love with a few souls so far," they said, and they buried their tongue in the golden-red sinews of my arcane liquidity while I ruptured beneath them with ecstasy.

When my hips stopped automatically jittering backwards I reached up and seized a fistful of their own soul. They moaned and tumbled to the stage and I pressed my open mouth against their hidden flesh.

Fists bang on the door. A key is scraped into the lock. On stage our tangled amalgam covers us in golden, fibrous starlight. The stage is flooded with antediluvian fluids spurting from secret apertures above us. A void has formed just above our souls, ink black and gently tugging at the curtains with its cold vacuum. Their sketches are curling in the warm gore on the auditorium floor. They whisper softly into the tender whorls of my wet non-binary soul, and I am luminous, golden, burning with their love and ready for our audience.

SCAPEGOAT

you can break a mirror
because it showed you the truth
but it will become

ten thousand truths

each one
sharper and deadlier than before

and   wilder

            in

design

ACKNOWLEDGMENTS

This book reached you because I had the love and support of my partners, specifically Afton Coombs and William Bibbiani. Thank you both for being in my life – my gratitude and love for you are boundless – having a mutual creative life support system really does help so damn much. A special thank you to my beautiful beta readers who have been with me for almost two decades now, Adam Trembczynski and Brian Künz; you're fucking real ones in a world that needs more real ones! Thank you to Joe Koch and Katrina Carruth, I'm grateful for your friendship, and for reading and encouraging me – you two are lighthouses in the horror community sea. Thank you to Sofia Ajram for the online movie nights – I appreciate your tolerance (and appreciation!) of my particular taste in films. And thank you to Sam Richard – for being cool as hell and believing in this book! Queer punks are the fucking best!!

PREVIOUS APPEARANCES

- "The Better Boy" originally published in *Sanitarium Magazine Issue 2*, May 2019
- "Neon" originally published in *Neon Horror: an Anthology of Terrors by Creators from the LGBTQIA+ Community*, June 2020
- "Hostile Architecture" originally published in *Antifa Splatterpunk*, January 2022
- "The Same Thing That Happened to Sam" originally published in *Your Body is Not Your Body: A New Weird Anthology to Benefit Trans Youth in Texas*, May 2022
- "The Thing That Moves the Meat" originally published in *Stories of the Eye*, October 2022

CONTENT WARNINGS

blood, drug use, manipulation, abusive relationships, child abuse/endangerment, bullying, implied sexual assault, implied assault, nonconsensual surgery, murder, physical assault, transphobia, cults, nausea/vomiting, incest, abortion, COVID

ABOUT THE AUTHOR

M. Lopes da Silva (he/they/she) is a polyamorous, bisexual, and non-binary trans masc author, artist, and critic from Los Angeles. He writes pulp and poetry. In 2020 Unnerving Magazine published his novella *Hooker*: a pro-queer, pro-sex work, feminist retrowave pulp thriller about a bisexual sex worker hunting a serial killer through the streets of 1980s Los Angeles using hooks as her weapons of choice. In 2022 Dread Stone Press published his first novelette *What Ate the Angels* - a queer vore sludgefest that travels beneath the streets of Los Angeles starring a non-binary ASMR artist and their vore-loving girlfriend - in *Split Scream Volume Two*. Book Slayer Press is scheduled to release his queer western splatterpunk novella, *On a Dead Horse*, in 2025.

ALSO FROM WEIRDPUNK BOOKS

Feral Architecture: Ballardian Horrors - edited by Sam Richard

J.G. Ballard has held a tremendous influence on culture since he first started writing, much of which turned out to be prophetic. In *Feral Architecture* Joe Koch, Donyae Coles, Sara Century, Brendan Vidito, and editor Sam Richard plume the depth of that influence through the lens of horror fiction.

The results are surreal, ominous, unexpected, unnerving, and a fitting tribute to the legacy of one of the 20th century's most impactful and important writers.

Featuring a foreword by Scott Dwyer of The Plutonian.

Elogona - Samantha Kolesnik

An evocative tale of sapphic love in a post-apocalyptic world dominated by religious zealots and supernatural monsters.

Kolesnik's *Elogona* transports readers to a time after the world's end, when a long-dormant sea creature has awoken to stake its claim against one of the last human settlements.

Verna must battle both man and monster to protect her family and her newfound love for Audrey, a refugee from the mainland.

Meanwhile, the Elogona calls...

"Otherworldly and grounded, immersive and gut-wrenching, *Elogona* feels all too real."

— RAE KNOWLES (*MERCILESS WATERS*)

Chaindevils - Matthew Mitchell

Embrace the chaos with Matthew Mitchell's debut novella, which tears off pieces of horror, grimdark fantasy, dying earth fiction, and drug literature, and smashes them together in hazy, mud-coated ways unlike anything you've ever seen.

"Mitchell pens a wild extrapolation of a post-apocalyptic North American Landscape by way of *The Road*, *Warhammer 40k*, and pulp westerns. *Chaindevils* is hard, grisly fare."

— LAIRD BARRON (*THE WIND BEGAN TO HOWL*)

Printed in the USA
CPSIA information can be obtained
at www.ICGtesting.com
LVHW021934011224
798045LV00035B/353